THE NEW DAWN THRONE

BLOOD MAGIC
BOOK SIX

JT LAWRENCE

FIRE FINCH

FIRE FINCH

 Created with Vellum

About the Author
JT LAWRENCE

JT Lawrence is a USA Today bestselling author
of 30+ books, and a Kindle Unlimited All-Star. Mother to a
menagerie of chaos, voracious reader, gin fan, and urban
farmer.

～

Stay up all night
with USA Today bestselling author
JT Lawrence.

www.jt-lawrence.com

amazon.com/author/jtlawrence

tiktok.com/@stay_up_allnite

instagram.com/authorjtlawrence

facebook.com/JanitaTLawrence

x.com/stay_up_allnite

bookbub.com/authors/jt-lawrence

pinterest.com/stay_up_all_night

linkedin.com/in/janita-thiele-lawrence-56533610

SPECIAL THANKS

*Immense gratitude to my readers
whose loyalty, support, and generous reviews
give me the courage to face the blank page
over and over again.*

I wouldn't be able to do this without you.

I hope you enjoy this new magical adventure!

- Janita (JT Lawrence)

THE NEW DAWN THRONE

THRONE

BLOOD MAGIC BOOK 6

CHAPTER I

THE MOUSE IS DEAD

"There's something else," said Morgan.

My brain was spinning like the Cup 'n Saucer ride at the Goblin City theme park. She went into the bathroom—a generous, beautifully designed room—and rooted around in the stylish laundry hamper.

"What are you doing?" I asked.

Morgan pulled out a small uniform with a badge sewn on the front pocket. ScreamCoaster, said the badge, and I knew immediately that it belonged to Nilve SaltySnap. But that didn't make any sense.

"Salty went missing in the portal," I whispered.

"Only according to the person who owns this *panic room*," said Morgan.

"Holy *faex*," I said.

"Look," she said. "Don't freak out. There's probably a reasonable explanation for this."

I glared at her. My intense feelings for Darick and the fairly damning evidence in the room were bashing up against each other and not making any sense.

"As I said before," she said. "I saw how he was with you. He was willing to go into that skyscraper filled with zombies to save you. When he saw you hurtling down to the concrete pavement he literally *stepped underneath* you to save you, even though it would have killed him if you—"

"What?"

"Jax. Do you know what I can't understand? If you had that cuff on when you jumped out of that window, then how did you slow your fall at the end like you did?"

I sighed, closed the closet, and moved to the chest of drawers.

"It's complicated," I said.

Usually I wouldn't search through someone's apartment on a first visit ... oh, who was I kidding? Of course I would. The first drawer held some gadgets. A remote control for a hidden-screen TV; an electronic reading device packed with books; a game console.

How long was Darick expecting me to stay?

"What do you mean, 'it's complicated?'" Morgan asked.

"There's a vampire," I said. "Lysander."

"Lysander?" she frowned, as if she recognized the name.

"We have a strange relationship."

"You *what*?" asked Morgan. "You have a relationship with a vampire?"

"It's not like that," I said. "I'm not attracted to him. But we do have this strange ... connection? A magical connection?"

I felt vulnerable saying it. Before then, I hadn't even admitted it to myself.

"Can you imagine having chemistry with someone but not in a sexual way?"

"Nope," said Morgan.

"He's not like the others. He's—"

"Don't tell me he's a good vampire. You've always said that there's no such thing as a good vampire."

I shook my head, pushing my hair out of my face. "He's not *good*. He's just ... different."

"Jax," she said. "What the hell are you trying to tell me?"

"When I was falling, I fainted. But just before that I felt something. I felt someone's arms 'round me."

"That was Darick," said Morgan.

"Before I reached the bottom," I said. "I heard his cape. I smelled his skin. It was Lysander."

Deep down I knew that Lysander had slowed my fall, saving our lives.

Morgan crossed her arms. "You're saying that a vampire—*an invisible vampire*—swooped in and cushioned your fall?"

"Believe me," I said. "Stranger things have happened."

"Have you mentioned him before?"

"Lysander?" I said. "No. I don't think so."

She narrowed her eyes at me. "There's something about his name."

I opened the next drawer. It was crowded with snacks of all kinds: Loopy Loops; Popping Ks; salt and vinegar potato chips; muesli bars; chocolate sticks; sour worms. It was as if Halloween had exploded in there. I hoped it wasn't a sign of things to come. I cleared my throat and slid the drawer closed.

Morgan clicked her fingers. "I've got it," she said. "I remember. His name was scribbled on the message at the desk."

"What?"

"At HQ. Someone phoned in a tip regarding your whereabouts."

"My whereabouts? When?"

"You remember when you stole Musubarin's laptop?"

"Borrowed it," I said.

She laughed. "Whatever. After Musubarin got out of that Laser Dungeon place he stormed into HQ. He was in bad shape, bruised and kind of manic. Anyway, I don't know what happened between you two down there—"

"He deserved it," I said.

"No doubt," said Morgan. "But he rolled into HQ calling for your head. He put out an APB, sent your photo to all available units, calling for your immediate arrest."

"And he changed the file," I said.

"Which file?"

"While I was trying to hack his laptop he remotely changed the schedule of the Ember Isles transfer to set a trap for me."

"Are you sure?" she asked. "He doesn't seem that clever, to be honest."

"Agreed," I said, and we smiled at each other, united by our intense dislike of a common enemy. "But when I arrived at the Crystal Clink, they were expecting me. They were ready with handcuffs and shotguns. It was a set-up."

Morgan crossed her arms. "I can't say I'm not impressed."

"I thought it was Musubarin, but when I mentioned his name to one of the guards there, she said that it hadn't been Musubarin who called in the tip."

"Lysander," said Morgan.

The deception stung. I thought Lysander and I had an understanding. "*Filius canis.* He was the one who set the snare."

Morgan scratched her head. "I still feel as if I'm missing something," she said. "What else do you know about this vampire?"

"Not much. He just showed up out of the blue a few days ago, around about the same time my life started to unravel."

Absent-mindedly, my hand flew up to the tattoo on my neck.

Morgan noticed. Morgan notices everything. It's the one drawback to having a detective as a best friend. "He knows you're a vampire-slayer?"

"As I said, it's complicated."

"He knows your parents were killed by vampires?"

"He knows more about my life than I do. He has this ... *file*."

"How?"

"I don't know. Because he keeps his friends close and his enemies closer?"

"Sounds legit."

"He knows my parents' names. Knows where I was born and what I weighed. He knew my freaking APGAR score."

"Congratulations," said Morgan, crossing her arms.

I frowned at her. "What?"

"You managed to not only have one obsessed stalker," she looked pointedly to the locked door, "but two."

"Argh," I said, rubbing my face. "Help me to understand what's going on."

"I'm just as confused as you are," she said. "But after Lysander tried to trap you at the Clink I'd go out on a limb to say that no matter how *complicated* your relationship is, he's not to be trusted."

"Yes," I said.

"What does he look like?"

I sighed. "Tall, athletic, blond. Like a supermodel, really. Intense eyes, like burning coals."

"Yep," said Morgan. "That sounds pretty complicated."

"And cheekbones," I said, sucking in my face and pushing in my cheeks with my fingers. "Incredible cheekbones."

Morgan stopped. "Say that again?"

"Cheekbones," I said. "Sharp enough to carve up a roast chicken from the Copper Cog."

"Shut up," she said.

"What?"

"Shut. Up." She started to tremble. It was slight, but I could see it. "I've seen him."

"What? Where?"

"Walk of shame," she said. "At my complex."

There was a whipping sound in my imagination. Durison's ghost may not be able to penetrate Darick's enchanted security system, but she was in my head, dressed up to the max in her dominatrix gear.

"Walk of shame?" I said. "Let me get this straight. There was a vampire supermodel creeping out of Liz Durison's house and you neglected to tell me?"

"I didn't realize he was a vampire. And I didn't know he had come out of Durison's house. I just saw him walk past. There was nothing suspicious about him."

"Oh my *faex*," I said. "Did you look into his eyes?"

"I may have," she said. "He's kind of easy on the eyes."

I rubbed my face again. "That's why you didn't report him. He mesmerized you."

"No, he didn't," she said. "Did he?"

"He planted the idea in your brain that there was nothing suspicious about him. So even though he was a complete stranger, and even though you found Durison dead, you didn't think to interrogate him, or even bother to mention him in the case report."

"Oh," she said. "That's how it works."

"Yes, that's how it works," I said. I was irritated, but it wasn't her fault. Just because I've never been mesmerized doesn't mean it didn't happen to others, and often. But more than the irritation was the flood of foreboding I was feeling.

"Hang on. Are we saying that Lysander is the V-Cult killer?"

I had invited the vampire into my home. Was I really that easy to fool? Maybe I wasn't impervious to mesmerization, after all.

"Bloody hell." Morgan delved into in her handbag. She pulled out Liz Durison's little black Flint book and paged to the last entry. She breathed out a nervous sigh and smacked the page with her palm, then showed it to me.

"Right in front of us," she muttered.

Rednasyl, the book said.

"It's all a bit backwards," the ghost of Liz Durison had mused that last time I saw her, lying on the lawn.

It was such a simple, classic code. Darick's words echoed in my head. When he gave me the password to the banking app on his phone, he had said *"The numbers are reversed."*

It's all a bit backwards.

Rednasyl. Lysander.

I hunched over and closed my eyes for a moment, and pinched the bridge of my nose. I had been so close to him. Under the influence of Vampire Venom I had offered my neck to him. I felt cold, cold, cold. Usually shame burns, but this was different. This was a cold terror edged with a kind of guilt I had never felt before. A cold serrated blade against my skin.

I remembered the photo he had shown me; of him standing in my kitchen. He had taken it with his phone. The same phone, I was certain, that he had taken the candid shots of me he had briefed Chuck Winnow with. The same phone that had my file.

"Why, though?" I asked. "Why kill all those women?"

"Psychopath," said Morgan.

"Why kill them and not me? And why save my life when I fell from the Carlton Centre?"

"Maybe he's obsessed with you. Maybe it's not fun to play cat-and-mouse when the mouse is dead."

"The symbol branded on the bodies," I said. "I found it in a book on ancient vampiric lore."

Morgan's eyebrows shot up.

"It's the symbol for the New Dawn. Hundreds of years ago, vampires used to rule the Realm. This book tells of a legend that the vampires will rule again. They call it the New Dawn."

Morgan stared at me without blinking.

"There's a group of vampires mobilizing. A powerful coven called the Silvano Clan who have been doing everything they can to restore that power."

"I know of them. But why now?" she asked. "After waiting for centuries?"

"There are three elemental fragments," I said. "If they manage to bring all three together they'll have the Black Fire: a power like nothing the Realm has ever seen. They'll be unstoppable. They'll probably wipe out every species apart from a few orcs for slaves and humans for bleed farms. It'll be the apocalypse. One of those fragments," I said, "the earth fragment, is the HighFire Crown."

"Which they already have."

"Exactly. When Estelar organized for the crown to be 'stolen' the word got out on the streets. The vampires jumped at the opportunity. If one of the elements was available, then they'd assume the other two were within reach, too."

"And are they?"

"The air fragment is the Chaos Jar," I said, and I brought it out of my pocket and set it down on the table between us.

"Oh," she said, her eyes, wide. "Oh. We're dead women walking."

I couldn't help but agree.

"The third?" she asked. "The third fragment?"

"I don't know. We didn't get that far. But I have to find it." I looked around at my high-tech prison cell, wondering how to get out. "It's the only way we can stop the prophecy from coming true."

As if on cue, the locks on the door clicked open, and I took a breath.

In strode Darick, with flames in his eyes, and at his side was Nilve SaltySnap.

CHAPTER 2

OLD APPLE

Despite my surprise at seeing Salty, I still noticed that Darick locked the door behind them. I had so many emotions running riot in my head I didn't know if I was Arthur or Martha. I shouted the prodigal goblin's name and ran to hug her. It was an awkward hug, and I came away a tad slimy, but I didn't care. I was so happy to see her safe.

"Where the *faex* have you been?" I yelled. "Darick told me you disappeared in the portal while you were rescuing Gizmo."

They both looked a bit uncomfortable then.

"What?" I said.

Darick rubbed forehead. "I—" he said.

Salty spoke at the same time. "We—"

I blinked at them. "I'm listening."

"That was what we agreed to tell you," the goblin said, carefully.

The betrayal was like a black hornet's sting. "You agreed to lie to me."

"We've got a lot to talk about," said Darick.

"How can I believe anything you say while you have us locked in here?"

Morgan chimed in. "Your kidnapping skills are on fleek, by the way. I had no idea I was being taken prisoner until you left the room."

"That's when we noticed the bars on the windows," I said. "The camera. The magical locks on the door. The security enchantment."

"It's for your protection," said Darick, and I gave him a look so scathing it could have set a forest on fire.

He grimaced as if I had slapped him. Maybe I should have.

"We can explain," said Salty. I gave her a withering look, too. Treacherous slimeball.

Darick looked at me tenderly, and it made my heart ache. "I've got so much to tell you," he said.

I thought of the bars on the windows and hardened myself against him. "Before either of you say one more word, I want my magic back."

Darick took forever to reply, and then he shook his head. "Sorry."

"I'm not kidding, *Darick*." I forced as much vitriol into his name as I could. "Give me my magic back."

"Please," said Darick. "Give me a chance to explain."

"Switch off your *faexing* force field, or whatever it is, and we'll talk."

I hated that. Hated speaking to him like that. Hated the feelings of betrayal and fear and confusion that felt like a whirlwind inside my body.

Most of all I hated the tainting of the honest relationship Darick and I previously had. Or the honest relationship I thought we had. Now it felt like a porcelain plate that had been smashed on the floor, Greek jungle party style, and even if we found all the pieces and glued them together, the cracks would still show. Forgiveness is one thing, but betrayal can never be forgotten.

Right then and there it felt as if my heart had shrunk to half its size. Shriveled like an old apple. I grieved for what I had lost. I had trusted him completely. I had fallen in love with him. I had imagined a future together where we could just be easy in each other's company, and more.

I felt like I hated Darick at that moment, but my desire for him was stronger than ever. I didn't understand the complexity of the feeling. All I knew was that I wanted him, and I hated him, and I wish we could just cut through all the terrible things swirling around us and just be. The plate may be broken, but love doesn't break. Love is not that brittle.

"Darick—" I said. But before I could finish my sentence he spotted the Chaos Jar on the table, and he looked at me in horror. SaltySnap saw it too, and swore like a goblin sailor.

"Jax," Darick said. He grabbed me by my arms, his fingers digging into my skin. There was electricity in his touch; his eyes were alight. I looked back, startled.

"Jax!" he said. "What have you done?"

CHAPTER 3
SIX FEET DOWN

"What have *I* done?" I asked Darick. "How dare you? I'm not the one holding two women hostage."

"I'm not holding you hostage," he said.

I looked pointedly at the bars on the windows.

Darick nodded. "It's for your own safety."

"I'm sure that's what Josef Fritzl said."

I expected him to get angry, or sigh in contempt. But there wasn't a trace of anything on his face but tenderness. His grip on my arms loosened, but he continued to hold me. I couldn't understand why, but my heart returned that tenderness.

"Please," said Darick. "I need you to listen. There are things you need to know."

We sat down on the pristine couches. The air was electric with tension.

"The jumpsuits hanging in the cupboard," I said. "The snacks. The gadgets. How long are you planning on keeping me here?"

"Until you understand what's at stake."

"I know what's at stake! The Silvanos are ushering in the New Dawn. The whole *faexing* Realm is at stake!"

I thought of Qwynkle, then, and thought he'd appreciate the pun—that of stakes and vampires. It made me glance at Salty, who had found said snack drawer and was helping herself to Loopy Loops and a game of *Were-Goblins in Space*.

"I was planning on keeping you here because no one can hurt you here. Just as you are not able to use magic inside, no magic can penetrate this enchantment from the outside."

"Okay," I said.

"It was my idea," said Salty, spraying us with multicolored sugar-coated crumbs.

"Sure it was," said Darick, giving the goblin an affectionate look.

"I said, let's lock her up somewhere," said Salty, "and then Darick said, '*Oh, I've got a panic room.*'"

"How convenient," I said.

"You won't hear me complaining." Salty tightened the belt on her robe. "It's like a five-and-a-half-star hotel."

"You've been staying here? In the panic room?"

"I have my own room," the goblin said.

I remembered how wealthy Darick was. "What? You own the whole floor?" I asked. I was kind of joking.

SaltySnap finished eating her Loops, scrunched the packet into a ball, and shot it up into the air. It landed in a small metal bin. "He owns the whole building," she said.

I don't know why I was surprised. I had seen his bank account. Darick was rolling in it; he had money raining down on his face. He had enough cash to lie down on the floor and make snow angels in it. I thought of all those large deposits I had seen listed on his banking app, all from the same benefactor, and it finally started to make sense.

"You're an assassin," I said.

Darick nodded. "Yes. I work for the Council."

Again, the feeling of bereavement came over me; that a patriarchal body I had respected my whole life had paid someone to kill me. It was difficult to talk past the lump in my throat.

"If the Council hired you to kill me," I said. "Why am I still alive?"

I'd seen Darick take people out. His technique was cold and clean and razor-sharp. If Darick wanted to kill me I'd have been tripping into the Afterlife.

"Why am I still alive?" I asked again.

Darick's stare was so intense I found it hard not to look away.

"I've been asking myself the same question," he said. "I've never failed to deliver on Council directives." He broke eye contact then and looked around the room, as if searching for a reason. "When the Council gave the command, I was ready to do it. I was given your details; your picture and address. Your routine. They must have had someone following you."

"Yes," I said, thinking of the deadling djinni, Alif Farzad.

"But as I watched you—"

"I knew you were stalking me."

"As I watched you I felt something. I felt like we were connected in some way. Then when you were attacked by those vampires outside Cucina Or'Capone I couldn't help myself. I needed to protect you."

"The Council must have been unhappy about that," I said.

"They soon stopped accepting my excuses. They wanted you dead, but I couldn't understand why. We're trained to follow orders and not ask questions, so when I approached them about your case they were incensed."

"They fired you?" I asked.

An ironic smile played on his lips. "The Council doesn't fire its agents."

His meaning was clear: no one gets to walk away from the Council. Alif Farzad could attest to that. There was one way out of the business arrangement, and that way was down. Six feet down. Things were starting to make sense.

"So that's why Musubarin's been so intent on getting you arrested," I said. "And that's why they were so adamant to get you on the Ember Isles ferry. Why they blew it up."

Darick nodded.

"Hold on," said Morgan, scratching her forehead. "Just hold on. The last time I checked, the members of the Council were supposed to be the most ethical people in the Realm."

"They were corrupted," I said. "I saw it for myself."

"But the whole point of the Council is to be incorruptible. High-principled. Beyond reproach, right?"

I shook my head. "I know. But I tested them, and they failed."

"What do you mean?"

"Wanting me dead is one thing, but when I gave them a notebook full of contacts of who were buying black magic market goods they destroyed it, right in front of me."

Morgan blinked at me. "I feel like my whole life is a lie."

"There was something about them," I said. "It was such an eerie atmosphere in there. Like they weren't themselves. Like they were all the same person. A vacancy in their eyes. I'm pretty sure they'd been mesmerized."

"That's what I thought, too," said Darick.

"Blimaex Abarim told them he was well again, and wanted to return to work, but they refused, and closed ranks. That's not how the Council should behave. When I went to the Winged Spire to give them the Chaos Jar the city was in total upheaval, and there was a crowd of over a hundred people waiting downstairs to see them. They were just hanging out in their suite, ignoring the phones and reading newspapers."

Morgan looked scared. "But how? How did the Silvano Clan mesmerize the whole Council?"

I shrugged. "They have the HighFire Crown. They have gallons of Magus. Their power is potent, and growing stronger by the day. They have a zombie army at their command, plus whatever is left of the Hammerskins to do their dirty work. At this point they can pretty much do whatever they like."

Her eyes were wide. "What are you saying?"

"We have to stop them," I said. "I just don't know how."

Darick cleared his throat. "My plan was to keep you safe here while I went after Acheron."

My anger flared up again. "*Filius canis,* Darick," I said. "I'm not your *faexing* damsel in distress."

"I know," he said.

"I'm not your princess that you can lock up in a *faexing* ivory tower—"

He shook his head. "I know, Jax, I know. I just—"

"Simmer down, wizard," said Salty. "He was just trying to keep you alive."

"I appreciate that," I said. "But—"

"But it's a moot point, now," said Darick, gesturing at the room and the locks on the door. "This doesn't matter. This won't protect any of us if we have the Chaos Jar."

We all glanced at the Jar at the same time.

"So, you're going to let me go?" I said.

"I was always going to let you go," he said. "I would have just preferred it if it weren't straight into the lion's den."

CHAPTER 4
THE WATER FRAGMENT

"So, what's the new plan?" Morgan asked.

"Talking of entering the lion's den ... there's only one thing to do," I said. "And that's to travel to the New Dawn Kingdom."

Morgan's face paled even more, and I felt my own skin grow white and cold.

"It'll be like that volcano pocket realm, if you can imagine that domain in its entirety. The volcano was a splinter of it, a fracture, as was Obsidian Hill. What we'll be entering now will no longer be fractured. It'll be an entire dominion that is totally controlled by the Silvano Clan. Their land, their rules."

"It's pretty much a suicide mission," said Salty, opening a packet of Popping Ks. Salted caramel scented the room.

"I agree," said Darick. "It's a death trap. But if we want any chance of survival, we'll need to unite the fragments before they do. It's the only way we'll be able to harness enough power to defeat them."

Morgan groaned and rubbed her face. Maybe she was thinking about her children, who would probably have to grow up without their mother.

"Look," I said to her. "You never signed up for this. You can stay here and watch the fort."

She laughed. "No way," she said. "No way I'm *not* going with you." She patted her holster, but her gun was no longer there.

"I have weapons," said Darick.

"I have magic," I said. "And a talented albino ferret."

"I'm the best Portal Magic goblin in the Realm," said SaltySnap.

It's an odd feeling, knowing you're going to seek out your own demise, and the deaths of the people you love. It was made slightly less odd by the knowledge that we had no other choice.

"I've never been to a pocket realm before," said Morgan. "Much less one run by the most ruthless vampire clan in the history of ever."

Nilve looked at her. "As Jax said, it's going to be enormous. Usually a pocket is a room, or a house—"

"Or a volcano," said Darick.

"But this is going to encompass Acheron's vision for his kingdom."

"A castle, then?" I said.

"Most likely. Vampires do love their medieval kingdoms."

I pictured a moat teeming with piranhas and ragged-tooth sharks, and boiling oil in cauldrons being emptied from above.

"What else?" I asked. "A forest?"

The Void knows I can't stand the idea of dark forests.

"Probably," said Salty.

Darick leaned forward. "It depends."

"On what?" asked Morgan.

"On what your experiences and fears are," he said. "A pocket realm will be a different experience for everyone. It's not a solid reality like this is." He banged on the armrest of the sofa. "It's fluid, and open to suggestion. My guess is that this particular realm will be able to draw on our fears and then make them come to life."

I felt sick to my stomach with nerves, and my mouth was dry. If I were to be one hundred percent honest, I didn't feel up to this particular suicide mission, especially if it was going to play on my worst fears.

"There will be a blueprint, obviously. A base. The castle, for instance, and the people there. That won't change. But there will be other things—"

"It'll be like an upside-down reality," said Salty.

"I don't really know what that means," said Morgan.

"You'll see," the goblin said.

"There's something else," said Darick. "Something I read in your dossier."

"What is it?"

"It's a bit of a bombshell, so I just want to prepare you, first. It's good news, but it won't be easy to hear."

"Tell me!" I said.

A bombshell? I'm ready.

"It's going to take every ounce of perseverance to get that crown," said Darick. "So maybe this will give you the extra strength you need to keep going."

"Oh for *faex* sake, Darick. Tell me already."

I realized I was cursing a lot but if there was ever a time to swear, it was then. Darick took my hand in his and squeezed it, as if to anchor me before his next words knocked me sideways.

"Your parents..." he said.

There was dead silence. There seemed to be no oxygen in the room. I forced myself to breathe; a long, slow, silent wheeze.

"What about them?" I asked, my voice sounding nothing like my own.

Darick squeezed my hand even tighter. His eyes and his grip were saying: *I've got you. You won't fall. I've got you.*

I gulped and repeated the question. "What about my parents?"

"I can't tell you if this is true or not, but it's definitely in your Council file. Jax, your parents are alive."

His words hung in the air, then dropped like a failed *Volas* spell.

I shook my head. "No," I said.

The Void knew I wanted it to be true. Wanted it more than anything in the world, but I saw them that day in their bedroom. Saw them lying drained and dead in their beds.

"I saw them—" I said. I looked at Morgan for reassurance, but she just covered her mouth, and her eyes welled up.

"You were a little girl," said Darick. "It was an extremely traumatic event. You were in shock."

I tried to wrench my hand away from him, but he hung on, despite the perspiration that began to cover my whole body. A cold sweat; clammy skin.

"I know what I saw," I said.

"They looked dead," he said gently. "They must have. Acheron was ambitious, even then."

My head was spinning. "Acheron? What does Acheron have to do with this?"

Then it was Darick's turn to look surprised. "You didn't know?"

"Know what?"

"The vampire that attacked your parents that day. What did he look like?"

I'd never forget what the man looked like.

"He looked like a vampire. Pale skin. Greased-back hair."

"And a scar on his forehead?"

Darick drew an imaginary line from his hairline down to his right eye, landing on the bottom of his eye socket.

"Yes," I said. Of course, I'd never forget that scar.

"You've never seen a picture of Acheron?"

"No." Vampires were notoriously camera-shy. It was a throwback from when there were mirrors in SLRs. And it's not like you could do an image search on Forage for it. "Are you saying that Acheron killed my parents?"

"They're not dead, Jax," he said, but I knew he was mistaken. I had known for twenty-something years that they were dead. I had woken with the knowledge and gone to sleep with the knowledge; an ever-present vacuum in my heart. *Orphanos.*

"Acheron was looking for the third elemental fragment," said Darick. "He found it in your parents."

"What?"

My head was spinning so fast I was glad I was sitting down. Darick never let go of my hand.

"Together, your parents had a special combination of blood. A potency that Acheron had never experienced before. Instead of killing them he took them with him so that he could—"

"He kept them alive?" I said. "All this time? They're still alive?"

My brain was not computing; my heart refused to hope.

"I know," he said. "It's a difficult thing to wrap your head around."

"Let's say you're right." It was almost impossible to fathom. "He's got them and he's using them for Blood Magic."

"Yes," said Darick. "That's what the file said. The Council tried to track him down for years but the magic he was siphoning from them kept him hidden. And he has slowly built on that invulnerability. He had a magic chamber, and he expanded that. Room by room. He began to broadcast his ambitions, and he gained a lot of followers. The vampires have been maligned for centuries. They want the Realm back, they want free rein, and Acheron promised to deliver that. Acheron had the water element fragment—your parents' blood—so he began to search for the HighFire Crown and the Chaos Jar."

"You said my parents have a special combination of blood. What is it?"

"That's something only they can tell you."

I stared at him with a mixture of tenderness and resentment.

"You've known this all along?"

Anxiety danced in my chest. Adrenaline; hope; fear.

My parents are alive.

My parents are alive.

My parents are alive.

"Since I read your file. Before I met you."

"And you didn't tell me."

"I knew what you'd do," said Darick. "You'd hightail it to the New Dawn Kingdom and get yourself killed."

I looked at Morgan, who shrugged. "He's right, you know."

"And now?" I said.

"And now you don't have a choice. But at least you won't be alone."

CHAPTER 5

JUST LOOKING AT THE STARS

"Okay," I said, standing up. "Okay. I'm ready. Let's go."

SaltySnap chuckled. "Oh, if only it was that easy."

"What are you talking about? You said yourself, you're the best Portaler in the Realm. What are we waiting for?"

"We need a location," said the goblin.

"We have a location," I said. "The New Dawn Kingdom."

"Without some kind of ... address ... I don't know how to get there."

"An address?" I snapped. "It's a pocket realm! It's in the sky somewhere. Upside-down. Inside out."

"Then you see the problem," said Salty. "My Portal Magic requires something slightly more concrete."

I remembered how we had found the volcano realm: Salty had used an envelope of the Belore twins which contained their savings, and had their handwriting on the front. The combination of Gizmo's ferreting skills and Salty's gateway magic did the rest.

"Gizmo will be able to find it," I said. "He just needs a clue."

Salty smiled, showing me her rubbery lips and dirty needle-teeth that I had grown to love. "A clue would come in handy."

"I have my mother's wand," I said. "And my father's pentacle ring."

"Good," said the goblin. "It's a start."

Darick shook his head. "Acheron has Jax's parents wrapped up in so many enchantments ... they're sure to throw us off."

"What about Lysander?" I said.

"Who's Lysander?" asked Darick.

"He's Jax's vampire boyfriend," joked Morgan.

"What?" Darick clearly wasn't in the mood for jokes.

"He's one of Jax's stalkers who just happens to be a serial killer," said Morgan.

"Can we be serious for a moment?" asked Darick. I'm not sure what made him feel on edge like that—the mention of a possible boyfriend or the fact that he was a serial killer.

"I am being serious," she said. "It's how this whole thing started. A couple of weeks ago I recruited Jax for a job that gave me a proper case of the creeps. I found my neighbor dead on her front lawn. She had a symbol branded on her chest—"

"The New Dawn symbol," I said.

"—and the weird thing was that she looked like Jax, lying there. And I got the fright of my life. Also there was this weird black mist everywhere, and it was cold, and the stars all disappeared—"

"What did you say?" I asked. "The stars?"

"The stars disappeared," she said. "I told you that."

"I know, it's just—"

Something nagged at me. My restless fingers found the ugly star charm on the bracelet that Darick had given me.

"Stars," I said, and they all looked at me as if I was on crack. I was just as confused, but my instinct was telling me something and I was trying to listen.

Stars. What about them?

All wizards that graduate from the Copperfield Institute have a thorough—and sometimes thoroughly useless—knowledge of astronomy, astrology, and space physics. Even though it was 2019, it was expected of wizards to be able to navigate their way using the stars. I guess having a Garmin named Sally didn't have quite the same gravitas.

The last time I had seen the ghost of Liz Durison she had been lying on that lawn again, her slowly decaying skin pale against the black grass.

"What are you doing?" I had asked her.

"Just looking at the stars," she had replied.

Then I understood that the bodies were not dumped arbitrarily. The stars were breadcrumbs.

"Morgan," I said. "Do you have a map of where all the V-Cult victims were found?"

"What?" she said, then, "Yes."

She took out her phone and pulled up a birds-eye view map of Johannesburg with red dots on it. I stared at it, trying to make sense of the shape of the dots. And then I saw it.

"It's a constellation," I said. I took her phone from her and enlarged the picture, drawing lines from dot to dot until I had the shape of Sagittarius. Only one star was missing: Nash.

"It's the centaur," I said. Like me, he was an archer, and he had drawn his bow. "Here," I said, and tapped the screen where the star was missing: the point of his arrow. That was supposed to be my dead body, right? That was where I was supposed to go. I superimposed the constellation over the map of the city to see where Nash would be.

"Where is this?"

Morgan zoomed in and copied the co-ordinates. She plugged them into her maps app and looked up at me.

"The Copper Cog & Ale," she said.

I swallowed hard. I was the final star, the final celestial body. Ferra's steampunk-themed pub for magical creatures was my very favorite place in the Realm. It was a poignant place for me. It was all about family and generosity and love and sustenance.

The vampires had chosen the perfect place for me to die.

CHAPTER 6
CRUSHED CATERPILLAR

D arick handed me a new pair of boots and fresh clothes to wear under my trench coat, then led us out of the panic room and down the passage, to another door. From what I could tell, his apartment was huge and minimally—but beautifully—furnished. Simple and stylish, exactly what you'd expect from a wealthy bachelor assassin. It was like a fancy hotel, if fancy hotels came with whole rooms of weapons. Darick welcomed us to choose whichever guns we liked. He preferred a sleek pistol with a silencer while Morgan was most comfortable with a Beretta, the same model she carried when she was captain of the Scorpions. They both inspected the weapons with practiced hands before holstering them. With a sparkle in her bulging eyes, Salty grabbed an AK47 and slung it around her potbelly, then stuffed her fanny pack with boxes of ammunition. If she'd have had a bandanna and some mud make-up, she would have looked like the goblin version of Rambo. Rambo in a hotel bathrobe.

"Ready?" I asked, and they nodded. Gizmo came running and leapt at me, giving me a hug before scuttling into my infinity pocket. I patted him through the Kevlar. I had the feeling he was going to come in especially handy on this trip.

To save Nilve's magic, we used the skeleton key to get to The Copper Cog. We huddled together in a circle and placed our hands on the key, and it knew immediately where to take us, as The Cog was where it originated. I closed my eyes, felt the comfort of the others' hands on mine, and I murmured the spell gently, hoping for an easy trip and a soft landing.

"Ianua sit," I said, and I felt the humming of the magic in my fingers and in my chest. It was so good to feel the sparks again that I almost lost track of the spell. I caught it in time and narrowed my focus, and soon we were all whipped up and away like paper dolls in the wind.

We LANDED EASILY and without much of a bump. SaltySnap's eyes clicked open and looked at me.

"You're improving," she said, which was high praise coming from one of the most talented Portalers in the city. My feeling of satisfaction only lasted a moment, though, because when we looked around and saw the destruction, our shoulders stooped. I felt as if all the burnt debris on the ground—all that was left of the wonderful pub and dwarf home—was actually inside my body, and my heart felt like a lump of cold ash. Morgan touched my arm, startling me, and I snapped back to reality. We had a job to do. This ruin, I promised myself, this devastation, would not be in vain.

I showed Darick the trapdoor that led to the underground hideout. It was still in place, so there was a good chance the Fernaks had survived the explosion.

Unless the gas leak got to them first.

I pushed that thought away and looked up at Darick. "Do you think we can open it?"

"We can try," he said, and began to look around for something we could use as a lever.

"I'll try Fig's workshop," I said. I wanted to check on the lab, anyway.

I made my way through what used to be the sparkling copper kitchen, where I always used to bump my head on the low archways and ceilings. Ferra's lab had not been spared by the explosion. Her expensive equipment lay destroyed. Although the air was clear, everything smelled of circuitry and old smoke. At my feet was the framed copper-wire embroidered quotation by Arthur C. Clarke. The frame was blackened, the glass cracked.

I couldn't help it. Hot tears sprang to my eyes and no matter how much I blinked, they kept coming. Irritated, I swiped them away. There was no time for weeping, no matter what we had lost. I could get rid of the tears, but not the heavy, swollen feeling I had in my heart. The truth was, I didn't want to be at that trapdoor when it was opened. I was petrified of what we might find there. I wouldn't be able to cope with seeing the Fernak family lying on the compacted soil floor. Wouldn't be able to live with the idea that I'd never see Ferra again, never feel one of her rib-cracking hugs again or hear her call me Jinxie.

I took a deep breath, forcing oxygen into my lungs to keep my mind on track. I was about to begin combing through the cinders when I saw in the corner—or what used to be the corner—some cabinets that were still standing. I opened them, not expecting to find much that hadn't been looted, but it turned out that no one had reached these one-touch doors. I didn't recognize most of the objects packed neatly in there, but I did recognize a gift that had been left for me. As the second drawer slid open, there lay a brand new crossbow.

I think Ferra had become so accustomed to me losing my bows that she always printed an extra to have on hand. I picked it up and kissed its lightweight frame.

Thank you, Ferra Fernak, I thought. *Dwarf surrogate mother, maker of magical crossbows, thank you.*

I checked that it was loaded and clipped it onto my back. As always, feeling the weapon pressing up against my spine fortified me. On my way back to Darick I walked through Fig's bombed workshop and swooped to pick up a metal shaft. I was trying to save up my magic for the battle, but if the lever didn't work I'd sling a *fiat fulgur* at the trapdoor to open it. Instinctively, and despite my reservations, I knew that the door was our way in, and our way out.

DARICK HAD FOUND his own tool and was using all his strength to lever open the trapdoor. I joined him, and with our combined strength we managed to break both levers, and the door stayed put.

"She put an enchantment on it," I said, reaching for my wand.

"Goblins are good at disarming dwarf enchantments," said Salty. She was looking more and more like a rebel jungle soldier now that she had soot on her arms and cheeks, and had swapped her robe for camo pants.

"*Now* you tell us," I said, stepping back with a sigh. Her lips crimped into a skewed smile.

Salty muttered a counter-spell in Goblin vernacular and there was a neat clicking sound, as if a key had been turned. I stepped forward to try the trapdoor again and this time it opened on command, as if it wanted us to enter. I was afraid to look down, and a flashback froze me in my tracks: the memory of stuffing Raguk Magra's body down the trapdoor in the bedroom at Alcazar. I heard the sharp crack his skull made as it hit the flagstone floor and a shiver ran through my body.

"I can't look," I said to Darick. He stepped forward and stuck his head through the opening in the ground.

"Dark," he said.

That wasn't a good sign. If the bulbs had exploded or the lights had burnt out—

Darick held onto the edges and lowered himself down into the fox den. Morgan stood next to the hole and called out, then threw down a flashlight to him. I heard him catch it, and turn it on. I still felt frozen. I heard him swear, and my knees turned to jelly.

No, I thought. *No, please, no.*

I clutched at my chest and found my father's pentacle ring there. I held it in my clammy fingers, hoping it would give me strength.

Please.

"And?" called Morgan, crossing her arms. "We're getting old here. What can you see? Is anyone down there?"

He swore again. I felt like melting down into the rubble. I batted away the imagined images of Ferra's children lying dead, gassed by a Hammerskin who had the intelligence of a crushed caterpillar. Just before I became overwhelmed by the emotions that were threatening to suffocate me, Darick called out.

"You've got to see this," he said.

CHAPTER 7
AT LEAST I WAS SHIVERING

We climbed down into the hideout and stared at the hole in the wall, which was lit up by the bright bulb of the flashlight in Darick's hand. All evidence pointed to the theory that the Fernaks and the Belore Twins had burrowed their way out of the den before the gas leak had reached them.

"How?" I asked, my body weak with relief.

Morgan examined the edges of the tunnel. "Some kind of boring machine."

I remembered the blueprints the kids had been working on when I had last visited them down there. There had been a pull-out of a magazine; an article on Elon Musk's tunneling technology.

We were quiet for a moment, savoring the relative happiness we shared that the Fernaks and the Belore Twins were probably alive and well. Then it was back to business.

"So," I said. "The missing star of the archer's arrow is here. There's a trapdoor, and a tunnel. I'm guessing this is the way to the New Dawn Kingdom."

If we followed the tunnel we'd probably come up somewhere dull and uneventful, like a nearby soccer field. But if we portaled to the pocket realm, my bet was that the tunnel would take us to Acheron Baldassare's castle.

"How do you know it will work?" asked Morgan.

"We don't," said Salty. "But it's the best plan we have."

"Plus, we have Gizmo," I said. "He's never let me down."

"Just remember," Darick said. "The parallel reality will feed on your fears. Don't give in."

"Ha," said Morgan. "Easy for you to say."

"Black mist," I said, more to myself than to anyone else.

"What now?" asked Salty.

"Directress Copperfield," I said. "She taught us to always consider the keel."

"I have no idea what you're talking about," the goblin said.

"Cold fire, dark bone, black mist. Always consider the trick, the turn, the twist."

"Still confused," said Salty. "Are you speaking in tongues?"

"She just meant nothing is as it appears. We should remember the flip-side. The *is* that *isn't*."

"But this whole pocket realm is the flip-side, right?" asked Morgan.

"Yes," said Darick. "So be on your guard."

"But how will we know what's real?" asked Morgan.

"Nothing," said Darick. "And everything."

"That's helpful," said the goblin.

"I know it sounds like a nonsensical riddle—" he said.

"It may feel like a dream, but it's not. If you die in a pocket realm, you die in real life, too."

I heard Morgan swallow hard, and Salty shuffled her feet. Anyway, what do you say to friends before embarking on a suicide mission?

"*Arrivederci,*" said the goblin, saluting us. "I'll keep the portal open for as long as I can. My personal record is two hours and forty-six minutes, so try to be back before then."

That would be virtually impossible. Time was not a solid construct in pocket realms. It stopped and started and yawned according to its own rules.

"We'll try our best," I said.

SaltySnap put her forearm out and we all grabbed onto it. Morgan and I exchanged a terrified smile, and Darick looked at me in a soulful way, as if he knew our time together was limited. Before I had time to say anything else the gateway spell was cast and we were hurtling through time and space. The air smelt of ozone. The northern lights flashed around us and the pressure squeezed our skeletons. The no-man's-land specters that were usually glued to the invisible portal tube were gone. Perhaps they'd found their way to the fracture in the Void and had escaped their lives of infinite banishment. Stars sparkled in my vision and my skin turned to braille.

Usually that is where the trip slows down and ends, but suddenly the trip turned cold—arctic cold—and so dark I couldn't see my freezing fingers in front of my face. My whole body started to shake and I lost feeling in my hands and feet, and then in my arms and legs. I could no longer move my fingers, and there was a kind of shooting pain in my face I'd never felt before. I was sure the blasting cold would stop my heart if I couldn't warm up soon. If I couldn't get some kind of break my body would shatter like a falling icicle when I landed on the other side.

That's when my lungs began to freeze from the inside. I could feel them hardening with ice dust like snowflakes, could feel them stop working as the cold shut them down, branch by branch. It became more and more difficult to breathe, and then it became impossible. I tried to wrap my arms around my torso. I tried to cough to wake my lungs up, but neither worked. I couldn't see my skin but I knew it was blue.

Breathe! I told myself, *Breathe!*

But my lungs were frozen slabs, no longer capable of expanding or absorbing oxygen. And just as I felt my consciousness fading, I was slammed to the ground.

I had arrived. I looked down at my body. It had not shattered.

Two things to be grateful for, I thought, as I lay on the hard floor, clutching at myself and shaking. At least I was shivering, I thought, my teeth clacking together. People dying of hypothermia stop shivering.

Once I had regained some small amount of body heat, I was able to move my previously paralyzed limbs, and I dragged my body up into a sitting position. I blinked into the darkness. I was in the hideout, all alone, and the tunnel gaped before me, like the mouth of one of those banished specters. I hated that I was alone. There was a camaraderie I felt when I was with the others, a feeling that everything was going to be okay. Of course, one of my greatest fears was being alone, dying alone, and the New Dawn Kingdom knew that. The pocket realm knew that an orphan's deepest desire is for love and companionship, and it had stripped me of that.

I was also keenly aware of the fact that my friends would be going through a similar rite of passage, facing their own fears, and my heart went out to them. This wasn't going to be an easy ride, but my desire to find my parents pushed me forward, just as Darick thought it would. I stood up, my rigid muscles screaming in protest, and stumbled over to the mouth of the tunnel. The dark maw loomed before me. It was a promise that I wasn't ready to hear. I climbed in anyway, and started crawling.

CHAPTER 8

GIANT SHARKS AND SNIPER BULLETS

I crawled through the tunnel for what seemed like hours. If the Silvano Clan's plan was to exhaust me before I ever got to the castle, it was working. As I crept and dragged myself along, forced into repetitive thoughts because of the sensory deprivation, my mind looped over and over, a spiral of dark ideas and flashing memories. Mostly, it was me struggling to accept the notion that my parents were alive. My memory of finding them dead was so clearly imprinted in my brain. Was it possible that I was wrong? And if they were indeed alive at that moment I found them, would I have been able to save them if I hadn't run away?

Instead I had slipped my dad's ring off his finger, and my mother's wand out of her hand; robbed them while they were just clinging to the edge of life. Fleeced them and ran away, an act of cowardice I'd never be able to forgive myself for.

You were a child, I argued. *A young traumatized child in an impossible situation. You thought they were dead. There is no need for guilt or forgiveness.*

And yet I had spent my days killing vampires in an attempt to spare the lives of their intended victims. I had spent years grasping at redemption.

Did killing vampires make me feel better? Sometimes, fleetingly. But the vindication was never complete. It was never something I could tick off my list. And I was just as lonely with or without it.

My bed was as cold.

Finally, there was the faintest lick of light in the distance. My knees were bruised and burning, shredded by stones, but I sped up, and it got brighter and brighter, until I reached the end, and climbed out.

THE DESTRUCTIVE THOUGHT loops were stopped in their tracks by the warm sunshine and the sound of waves crashing on the beach. Golden sand and palm trees glittered under the brilliant blue of the sky and I could smell the salt on the warm ocean breeze. It was an island paradise, but it would not fool me. I was in Acheron's lair. It looked like a sprawling, silver-sand utopia, but I felt the evil vibrating in the air around me. It's a difficult thing to explain to someone not accustomed to feeling the magical vibrations of a place. Morgan had described it as an invisible black mist. I feel it as a slight pressure, a gelid doom closing in on me, fraction by fraction.

When I had stood outside Slyden Abarim's house I had experienced a similar feeling; the knowledge of the darkness that is waiting to swirl around you. I had described the house as having been turned upside-down and dipped in evil. Acheron's pocket realm felt the same. It looked like a paradise, but I knew better than that. I was not going to let my guard down. I shielded my eyes from the glare of the sun and looked up; I saw something that made me realize that it wasn't any old island I was standing on. A huge tower loomed before me.

The pocket reality resembled the world I knew, and that was scary enough without it echoing the very worst parts of the Realm. I stared up at the Black Tower, dread cascading like cold water inside my body. I was standing on Ember Island.

I didn't want to approach the building—I knew full well that interlopers were shot on sight by a band of marksmen with sniper rifles—but I didn't know what else to do; I didn't know why I was there.

I felt Gizmo move in my pocket and felt a small measure of relief. He would show me the way. His head appeared, and I stroked him. The sun seemed to grow in size, and the bright light hurt my eyes. The rays were beating down on us.

"What are we doing here, Gizmo?" I asked.

Wasn't it just the way the pocket realm was designed? To confront you with every fear you had. As if on cue, I looked out toward the ocean and saw a giant shark fin cutting through the water. It looked like a Megalodon was swimming determinedly back and forth, waiting for me to enter the waves.

It will feel like a dream, SaltySnap had said—and it did—*but if you die in the pocket realm you die in real life, too.*

Giant sharks and sniper bullets. Basically it was like a nightmare, but worse, because the stakes were real.

I STARTED HEADING in the direction of the tower, following Gizmo's nose even though my body was saying *Hell No.* I needed to move, and the albino compass was never wrong. I needed to gain ground and get to Acheron's castle. I began to walk toward the center of the island, which bristled with sharp rocks and palm trees. It was good to get away from the sun; I could feel the heat of the sand through my boots, but the steaming jungle air was hardly a relief. I took a closer look at one of the large black outcrops and recognized the form. They were volcanic rocks, and the prolific plants racing around them and all over the island were the same kind of plant that had eaten my kitchen whole. Of course the Ember Isles were volcanic islands. It all tied together with the fractured realm we had visited to save the kidnapped Belore twins. Acheron had spent decades constructing this neat little reality for himself that stacked together perfectly. Neat for himself, that is, and his clan. Deadly for us.

I kept going, fighting the heat and the tendrils of the plants that seemed intent on tripping me up. I wasn't sure if they were being spiteful, or trying to save my life. Eventually, the plants got their way, and I stumbled and fell.

It was a soft landing. The beach sand had given way to moist soil churned up by roving plants and animals. I stood up, dusted myself off, and continued in the direction of Gizmo's snout. It felt then as if the island was alive, that it had its own consciousness and agenda. I wasn't sure if I was imagining it, but it began to feel as if it were tugging at me. Perhaps it was just anxiety, or exhaustion, but it soon felt as if the earth was sucking at me, pulling my shoes down into its soft soil.

Now, I had watched enough 1980s horror films to know that sinking sand was a common threat, so I didn't ignore the signs. I picked up my pace. Perhaps if I was fast enough I could outrun the danger. The Tower was a massive building and there was no way it was built on shifting sand. The land would be solid there. It became like one of the dreams where you run and run and you don't get anywhere. I kept going, but soon there was more quicksand than there was anything else, and I hopped onto a black rock. While I caught my breath, I wondered what the hell to do.

It felt pretty hopeless. I was hot and thirsty, and my calves were burning.

That's when the Komodo dragons showed up.

CHAPTER 9
BARBECUED WIZARD FOR BREAKFAST

Seriously? I thought. *Komodo dragons?*

If there ever was an animal that suited vampires it would be the vicious blade-toothed Komodo. They're cold-blooded carnivores who eat their young.

At first there was just one, and it shuffled toward me on its reptilian legs, swiping its tail from side to side in a sinister way. I thanked the Void for the rock I was standing on, but I knew my advantage would not last long. More hungry lizards appeared and they all moved toward me as if I was the tastiest looking turkey they'd ever seen. The closest one —the first one I had spotted—was at the base of the rock now, trying to climb up. More than twenty others followed it from all directions, and soon I was surrounded by the sweeping black-tongued reptilians. Fear flared inside me.

I didn't want to reach for my crossbow. I didn't enjoy harming animals, even those that wouldn't think twice about eating one of my legs for dinner. I unclipped my wand instead.

I took a deep breath, and tried to direct my adrenaline in a way that I could focus my energy on building my magic. I felt the fear in my heart and my throat, and I welcomed it and turned it around in my chest, forcing it to transform from fright to power. I pointed the wand at the climbing creature nipping at my boots. It was about to sink its deadly teeth into my ankle. I felt the magic whooshing through my chest and forearms, felt the sparks glitter over my skin.

"Glaciem exquiris!" I shouted, and a thin stream of icy blue light shot out of my wand and slammed into the dragon, freezing him.

The animal grunted and fell backward, onto his team mates, who scattered and hissed. They didn't retreat. If anything, they seemed angry that their snack on a rock had turned problematic. I lifted my wand again, but the dragon I was aiming at shook its head and breathed a column of orange fire at me.

Shocked, I slapped the flames off my arms. It was too late to save my eyebrows; I had the feeling I wouldn't need to pluck them any time soon, or ever again.

What the faex? I thought. *Fire-breathing Komodo dragons?*

I didn't know whether I should be appalled or impressed. Either way, if I didn't get out of there, pronto, the lizards would be having barbecued wizard for breakfast.

They kept advancing, and struggling to climb up the steep corners of the rock.

"Nano, fireproof helmet," I said, and my nano snaked out of my pocket and formed a dense, compact helmet around my head.

"*Glaciem exquiris!*" I shouted again, knocking the closest one off the rock. He dropped with an evil-sounding squeal. As before, the magic made them angry, and I was treated to some lizard-breath fireworks. This time I was prepared, so I dodged the worst of it and my nano protected me from the rest.

"*Glaciem exquiris!*"

I knocked another one off just as it was about to skewer my calf. There was a part of me that was repulsed and afraid of the creatures snapping at my heels, but another part of me reveled in the battle. It was so satisfying to have my magic back and to be able to defend myself.

I was able to freeze every one of them and had hardly a scratch to show for it—that's if you ignored the new eyebrows, or lack thereof—and soon I was able to climb down from the lava rock and pick my way through the scaly pale-bellied bodies. Of course, this didn't solve the problem of the sinking sand, so my elation at winning the struggle against the reptile rebellion was short-lived.

I couldn't figure out how the rocks weren't sinking, nor were the Komodos. It was as if the sand wanted to swallow me in particular. Which didn't make any sense until I remembered that this wasn't just any island. This particular obstacle course was very personal. Again, I tried to outrun the sucking soil, again it tripped me up, as if I had been caught in the spin cycle of a fantasy nightmare.

It latched on to me. I had entered the vortex of the widening gyre. At first it was just a foot, and I didn't panic. It was just a foot, after all. A slab of meat and five toes. I could get on pretty well with just one, I was sure. But then it was up to mid-calf, and no matter how much I struggled and kicked and pulled on a nearby tree root, it kept sucking me down. When it reached my other foot, and swallowed my leg just as quickly as it had the other, and I before I knew it, I was waist-deep in the sand.

I remembered an old childhood conversation. Another kid, presumably a street urchin, had told me that the more you struggle, the deeper the sand pulls you in. I understood the warning, but I failed to see what the alternative was. So I continued to struggle and kick against the sand as it vacuumed me into its abyss, and indeed the more I kicked, the more it seemed to grip me. I yelled out in frustration and looked up at the plants and saw vines like ropes.

"*Volas!*" I shouted, and the panicky feeling inside me reached out and grabbed the strongest-looking vine I saw, and brought it down to me. I put my wand in my mouth and grabbed the rope with both hands and started climbing it. The soil refused to let me go, but I put all my strength into inching up that vine. Every centimeter was a victory. I kept on and on, till my forearms and thighs cramped, and I slid down, losing a hand's-width of hard-won progress. I clung on, waiting for the muscles to release, and then climbed again. The vine was taking strain. I heard it cracking above me, and I had no choice but to climb harder and faster even though my muscles were on fire.

Finally I was free, and I jumped away from the eddy of hungry earth, onto a raft of palm leaves nearby, and I kept running. I had to get away from the quicksand. I knew I didn't have the strength to climb out again.

I RAN AND RAN, dodging the sharp black rocks and suspicious sand pools until I was deep into the tropical jungle. While I was running, I was thinking what a right *filius canis* Acheron Baldassare was. So he knew I was scared of Ember Island, but that wasn't enough for him. He had to add some sharks and fire-breathing lizards and sinking sand to the mix.

When I reached the perimeter of the tower I was aching and out of breath. The canopy of the plants protected me from the sniper's view. The building was vast, and I put my palm on the wall to rest.

I was immediately sorry. It felt strange to the touch, and I flinched and snatched my hand back. When I looked closer, I saw that the wall was made out of human bones.

The sinking sand was no unhappy coincidence. It was designed to swallow you. The Komodos were carnivorous, but so was Ember Island.

CHAPTER 10

SWARM OF SHARK FINS

The island was designed to eat people and use the bones to grow the tower. I shuddered. I saw an eye socket; a bleached jaw bone; a femur, still dirty and fresh-looking. Who needed snipers when you had a whole island ready to consume you? I had to get out of there, but I didn't know how. Then I remembered the underwater caves that Darick had pulled my limp body to, the last time we were in the area. It wasn't an ideal solution. I had Gizmo in my pocket, and as far as I knew, magical albino ferrets didn't know how to swim. Also, there was at least one shark trawling the waters there, and the beast was the size of a small country. It wasn't a good solution at all, but it was the only one I had. I walked past the tower and kept going, happy to leave the hungry lizards behind, and hoping no new surprises were waiting for me on the other side of the island. I saw evidence of more nightmare fuel: a shed snake-skin that was wider than I was tall, bubbling pits of who-knows-what, and, when the jungle fell quiet, a faint shuffling sound behind me. Paws on leaves. Panting. Somehow I knew the sounds did not belong to a border collie that had come to save my life.

I fought my way through the jungle, sweating and itching, looking forward to the cool relief of the seawater that would soon be on my skin. But when I got to the beach, the shark fins had multiplied. There was no way I could enter that water without being instantly turned into ceviche.

Faex! I thought. *This island is not going to let me go.*

I wondered then if I would be able to conjure up a speedboat. It would take a heck of a lot of magical energy, but if I could pull it off, I'd be able to skip over the waves I was looking at and head to the nearest non-carnivorous coast.

I was still holding my wand, which I had—against all odds— not lost to the quicksand. I clutched it in my palm and took a breath to steady my nerves. I wasn't very good at conjuring up objects, and I didn't know a lot about sailing, or boats, but I tried to picture one with a pretty solid hull—to protect against inquisitive sharks—and a powerful engine.

"*Evoco et excito, nunc et semper, res ac mortales: navia.*" I said, and a beautiful white speedboat appeared. It had blue and silver lines around the edges, like the ocean at sunrise. It seemed too good to be true, but that didn't stop me from pushing it into the water and climbing in. I turned the key and released the lever, and the engine came to life. I could smell the gasoline in the warm air and it made me feel nauseated. I hoped our next destination wasn't too far away. I could feel the conjuring magic drawing my power every moment the engine was purring. I kicked it up a gear. The faster we went, the cooler and fresher the air was, and the better I felt. I could taste the sea salt on my lips.

"Nano, buoyancy vest," I said, and my nano formed a neat little black waistcoat that wrapped around my torso and inflated. I patted it, to make sure it was tightly fitted, and accelerated more.

"*Hasta la vista,*" I said to the swarm of shark fins. "No Jax-flavored ceviche for you. Not today, anyway."

I glanced back at Ember Island, happy to be leaving it in my toxic fumes. There was a charcoal gray wolf sitting at the water's edge, his hungry bright green eyes glowing against his thundercloud pelt.

CHAPTER II

THE CORPSE ON MY LAP

We arrived at what looked like the coastline of a large piece of land, and I was happy with that. I'd had enough of islands. The land was dark with trees; tall conifers that cast so much shade it looked like nighttime when you stood beneath them. I jumped out of the boat. I was grateful for it, but would be happy to see it turn into white smoke and disappear so that it no longer drew on my energy. But Instead of it vanishing, it turned into a white palomino. The horse's mane had the same silver and blue highlights as the speedboat had. I looked at him uncertainly. I knew less about horses than I did about sailing. I really needed to work on my expensive-hobby repertoire.

"Hello," I said, and the pale horse snorted. I thought about trying to make him disappear into the white smoke I was going for before, but it seemed mean to conjure up a creature and then smoke him. Besides, a horse could come in handy in this kind of forest. My body was exhausted from my earlier struggles, and I could do with a lift.

"Nano, saddle," I said, and my nano swept over to the horse and turned into a neat black saddle.

"Right," I said, to no one in particular. I wasn't sure of the etiquette involved in climbing onto a strange horse. It seemed rude to just clamber on. Didn't I need some kind of introduction? A sandwich, perhaps, or a sugar cube. I approached him slowly, and put my hand on his flank, stroking him and speaking gently. He didn't seem to mind me too much, so I put on my big girl panties and placed my foot in the stirrup, then grabbed onto him and hauled the rest of my body over, finding the saddle comfortable and the reins soft in my hands.

Before I had the chance to say giddy-up the palomino swung his head and started trotting into the forest, which was dark, eerie, and calm.

NO FREAKS OF NATURE HERE, I thought, then immediately regretted it. I didn't want to jinx the new landscape or my new ride.

We moved further into the forest. It was cool and scented with pine. I wondered where Darick and Morgan were. I'd have felt a lot more comfortable with them by my side. Salty was holding the portal open for us. I had no idea how to find it in this shifting-reality realm but I pushed it out of my mind. *Hakuna Matata.* I would worry about that later. We had decided Salty should stay and keep the gateway open for two reasons. The first was for her safety and ours: if something happened to her in the New Dawn Kingdom, we'd never be able to get back to the Realm. The second was that an open portal was like a siren to other magical creatures. There was the chance that friends of ours would hear the call and come through to help us. The Khargols had done this when we had been trapped in the volcano pocket, and I hoped that at least some of them would come through for us again.

We traveled further into the woods, and I enjoyed the sensation of being higher up than normal, and appreciated the horse doing the work while I rested. My hips moved in that lazy way horse-people's do when they're out for a stroll in the saddle. The woods got darker, and I had the intense feeling of *deja vu* settling on my shoulders like a cold mantle. What was it about sinister forests? And then I came to a clearing and understood the feeling of familiarity of these particular trees. The slate-colored Gallanrock stood in the middle of the circular glade. It was Brimware Grove, where the StarDust Coven were tricked into coming for their Spring Equinox Hexenwald. Hazel Shackleton had been hanged by the neck from the top of the trees that formed a huge birdcage around the sacred rock.

The memory turned real. Suddenly I saw her body hanging there, her limbs heavy, her face slack. Her chalky skin was blistered with the beginning of putrefaction. I tried to blink the disturbing memory away, but could not. The specter remained. Something touched my shoulder and I jolted. I spun the horse around, expecting to see the face of Ophelia

Knox, but instead I saw a flash of black. I turned the horse around again, and saw Shackleton open her eyes.

I blinked again, trying to see clearly, trying to see the forest for what it was, instead of a bad dream forged from my memory that day. But Shackleton's body remained strung up. Her hands traveled to her neck, and she kicked, as if she were trying to break free. I knew she was dead; could see she had been dead for days, but I scrambled off the horse and ran to the rock. I climbed it and reached out for her, expecting my hand to come away empty, but her body felt as real as mine. Once I had a grip on her full black skirt, I pointed my wand up to the rope and shouted *"Ignem Exquiris!"*

The fear in my body focused into a white laser and quickly cut through the noose, bringing Hazel's body slamming down onto mine. I absorbed the hit, only just keeping my balance, and then slowly and carefully carried her down to the ground. I saw the flash of black again, and this time I was not frightened. A raven landed on the top of the rock, and I knew it was Kresnik.

"Bron!" I said, and the bird nodded and kwooked. His head twitched from side to side. I was so happy to see him, even if he was still stuck in his avian form.

Bron screeched, making me jump. I looked down at the corpse on my lap, and instead of seeing Shackleton's face, it was Ophelia Knox. She smiled at me, then smashed her wand into my face, swiping me sideways onto the forest floor. My wand disappeared into the carpet of leaves. It happened so quickly I barely registered it. All I knew was that Ophelia was standing above me in that spooky wedding dress of hers, and I was at her mercy. Or, at least, she thought I was at her mercy. The raven flapped his wings and flew around us, trying to distract the witch. Ophelia swatted at him, but he was faster than her, and managed to draw blood from her face. She cried out and wiped her dead-skin cheek, and her fingers came away black. Her eyes widened and her mouth shrank in fury. Instead of wiping the blood on her dress, she put it on her other cheek, so that she looked like a warrior.

A black feather lay at her feet. She bent to pick it up; I imagine she wanted to put it in her hair to save it for later, when she could use it for some cruel Contagious Magic.

"No!" I said, scrambling forward and getting to the feather first. I sprang up and with trembling fingers I shoved it into my pocket. "Change him back," I said to Ophelia. "You've had your fun. Change him back to his human form."

I hated asking, but as the issuer of the original spell, she was the only one who could release him from it.

She looked amused. "Why would I?" she said, and then her features darkened. "I asked you for help the other day. You didn't oblige. So why would I do anything to help you now?"

Ophelia and Dylan Knox had been on the ferry that was bound for Ember Island.

"I didn't know," I said. "I didn't know it would blow up."

"Oh, it's all right," she said, smoothing the decaying flesh of her cheek back in place. "I never did worry about the little things."

CHAPTER 12
GIANT BIRDCAGE OF FIRE

Bron landed on the ground and called loudly to me. He'd spotted the silver of my wand peeking out from the leaves. I twirled and scooped it up, then found steady footing. I pointed the wand at Ophelia. Or Ophelia's ghost, or zombie, or whatever she was in this strange nightmarish kingdom.

She laughed at my wand. "Do you think your magic is a match for mine?"

"No point in guessing," I said. I could feel the current building in my arm.

"You don't belong here," the witch said.

"Nor do you. You're dead," I told her. Not that she needed me to point it out. I'm sure she could feel the way her skin was sliding slowly off her skeleton. "In fact," I said, "I don't understand why your exploded bones are not lying at the bottom of the ocean."

She hissed at me then, like a snake. I wasn't expecting it, and it sent my heart racing. Her lips and eyes were shiny black, and her hair turned into a nest of baby vipers. The palomino spooked and galloped into the forest, taking my nano with him. I began to feel cold and stiff, as if she was freezing me with the sibilant sound that was coming from her. My body felt numb, like I would never feel or move again.

The magic shot out of my wand almost of its own accord.

"Fiat fulgur!" I shouted, and my words joined the streak of magic just in time, slinging the lightning bolt into Ophelia's chest. She screeched—a sinister, otherworldly sound—and the squirming snakes died away into ash, a gray powder that dusted Ophelia's shoulders. Her mouth was wide open, a screaming black vacuum that threatened to swallow me.

"Fiat fulgur!" I yelled again, and sent another bolt of lightning into her, cracking open her chest with its hot white light. She fell backwards, arms out, palms up; she landed hard, scattering decaying leaves in a halo around her. A black cloud of bats erupted from her open ribcage and flew up in my direction, screeching in the same way as Ophelia had before I'd skewered her with my lightning.

The bats attacked me, tearing at my face and tangling my hair. Bron tried to protect me, but there were too many of them. I screamed and dropped my wand again, and heard my shriek echo in the dark forest. I felt their dirty claws needling my skin and I felt like they were inside my body, too, because I couldn't get a grip on my thoughts or my magic. I couldn't see the ground, couldn't see anything except the flutter of the leathery wings and menacing eyes. I wrapped my arms around my head, trying to protect my face from the worst of it, worried they'd damage my sight.

Fire, I thought at last. *Fire should scare them.*

"Ignem exquiris!" I shouted, and the ground before me caught fire. It didn't seem to bother the bats, who kept dive-bombing me and lacerating my neck and cheeks.

"Ignem exquiris!" I shouted again, and a new patch of ground lit up. I dropped down, desperately searching for my wand. I had to take my hands away from my face and I felt the animals all over me, even brushing my lips and inside my ears. A new boost of adrenaline kicked in. I found the wand, warmed by the flames.

"Ignem exquiris!"

This time the flames shot out like a comet towards the creatures, and a good portion of them screeched and fell to the forest floor. The fires on the ground were spreading, and one had reached the natural gazebo, licking at the base of its trunks. The fire grew, and finally the bats flew off, into the dark. I realized too late that I was surrounded by fire, the same fire that was slowly consuming Ophelia's broken-open corpse.

WHEN WOULD I learn to avoid using magic when I was not in control of my emotions? It had almost killed me a couple of weeks ago, battling Qwynkle, and now I'd painted myself into a corner of flames.

Q: What is worse than a spooky forest?

A: A spooky forest on fire.

I could feel the heat of it then, like a waterfall of lava, and I was reminded of the volcano realm, and the speeding steam train that had careened into the mountain. The bonfire where Ophelia had tried to burn Crowe and I alive.

Was I destined to die in a fire? Surveying my surroundings, it certainly looked like it. It was gaining momentum; orange walls surrounded me, and I had no choice but to run through the tall flames and parkour up onto Gallanrock, where the heat was unbearable and made the air shimmer all around me. Bron circled above, calling and calling, but there was nothing he could do. I could feel Gizmo squirming in my pocket. My trench coat was fireproof, but he could feel the heat that was threatening to eat us alive.

My favorite spell had always been *ignem exquiris*. I loved the feeling of being able to harness such a potent element. But standing on that rock and feeling the heat broiling my cheeks, I remembered that old saying: *Live by the sword, die by the sword.*

Fire was my sword.

My skin was searing hot, and my legs were beginning to burn. The flames climbed the twelve tall trees that formed the gazebo around me, higher and higher, till it looked like I was being held captive in a giant birdcage of fire.

CHAPTER 13
MALICE IN UNDERLAND

When I heard the galloping, I thought I must have been hallucinating from the heat. But when I looked up, I saw the silver-white horse racing toward me. Someone was on his back but I couldn't see who through the shimmering wall of fire. It was an arresting thing to behold, the handsome quicksilver steed crashing through the flames to rescue me. If I was dreaming, it was a beautiful dream.

"Jump!" yelled a woman's voice, and I steadied my legs, waiting for the horse to get close enough. I pushed off with all my might and flew through the air, which was so hot I thought it would burn my lungs. I landed behind the rider, quickly righted myself, and clutched her designer-cloaked waist while the horse whinnied and raced, hooves thundering against the crackling fire below. Isadora Crowe handled the animal like an expert horsewoman, negotiating a path away from the blaze. She maneuvered around the rocks and tree trunks we could avoid and jumped over the obstacles we couldn't. I held onto her body. It was taut with tension but at the same time I sensed an ease that I guessed came with being a natural horsewoman.

We finally reached the end of the ever-growing circle of flames and she allowed the horse to slow to a canter, and then a trot. Once we were out of danger, she instructed him to stop, and she climbed off and dusted her hands, then patted his neck.

"Good work," she mumbled to him. "Good work, boy."

I climbed down too—although, it must be said, not as elegantly as Crowe had done—and watched as the witch inspected the horse's body. His hooves had protected him from the worst of it, but his legs were still blackened. I felt terribly sorry for him and wished I could take the scorch marks away. Izzy saw the look on my face.

"Don't worry, he'll be fine. We'll find him some water."

"Where did you come from?" I asked. "I thought I was hallucinating when you arrived like a knight in shining armor."

The bottom edges of her cloak were blackened, the stars in the fabric continued to pop and fizz.

"I saw the portal open at The Copper Cog," said Crowe. "Salty said you were here."

"But how did you find the forest? Nothing makes sense here."

I felt like I was the main character in *Alice in Wonderland*, although there was very little wonder to be found here. Perhaps *Malice in Underland* would be more fitting.

"I felt Ophelia's presence," said Crowe. "I was drawn to it. I never had the chance to finish what was started at the Moonlit Chapel. She ran away from us before I had time to disperse her evil."

"Well," I said, gesturing at the fire behind us. "Ophelia's energy has officially been dispersed."

Isadora looked at the cuts on my cheek. "I knew you two were bound to battle so I came here to perform the *Hexenwald* and finish the job."

"Thank you," I said. "That was the second time I was almost barbecued today—"

"Just returning the favor," she said. "And Ophelia got what was coming to her."

"Why are dead people here?" I asked. "Is it like some kind of purgatory? Ophelia was on the ferry when it exploded. I saw her handcuffed inside the transfer van."

I didn't get it. I thought the new dawn kingdom was all about Acheron and his evil castle in the upside-down sky. I wasn't counting on bumping into the killers of Halloween past. If dead people had free rein in this realm then I was going to be in a lot of trouble. I already had enough *breathing* people trying to kill me, thank you very much. I didn't need to add the undead to that list. The idea of a zombie Qwynkle—or Slyden Abarim—sent fear zipping through my body.

Crowe shrugged. "I don't know. Maybe Ophelia made some kind of deal with the devil."

"Let's hope that's the case," I said. "Or I may as well march right back into that fire."

The horse whinnied and pranced. The flames were approaching again and he wanted to get away.

"We'd better get out of here," I said. Crowe agreed and gently held on to the palomino's reins, driving him forward into the cooler air. "He's a handsome one," she said, stroking his flank. "What's his name?"

"Er…" I said. *Speedboat?* Then I looked at his mane which shone with its silver highlights. "Quicksilver."

Isadora nodded and smiled. "He's a beauty."

CHAPTER 14

A TRICK FOR A TRICK

We walked deeper into Brimware Grove, where it was so dark it was like night. As we approached the far edge of the forest it started getting lighter again, and the air smelled less and less like pine. I recognized the building that appeared in the distance. It was the pavilion at the Great Oaks Medieval Faire.

"Oh, great," I snarked. "We're back at the Faire."

The setting brought back harrowing memories. Our last visit here had not been pleasant. We had lost a member of Crowe's coven, and Bron had witnessed it. He had subsequently been hexed into his raven form, a spell I couldn't reverse.

The building was deserted, but we managed to find an old ice bucket which I filled with water for Quicksilver. When he had quenched his thirst I threw some water on his forelegs to cool them down, and I noticed the scorch marks were permanent. A mark of valor he'd carry forever.

I commanded the nano to retire to my pocket, which it did, and we all trudged toward the center of the grounds, where the festivities were usually held. There was no one in sight. The grass was dead and dry and the storm clouds rolled in, rumbling above us in a threatening way. The wind picked up, disturbing the palomino, and I felt unsettled, too.

Within moments of the heavy clouds appearing, the sky opened up and pelted us with rain. Every time lightning struck, Quicksilver reared up. Crowe suddenly looked worried, and frowned at something in the distance.

"What is it?" I shouted, but she just shook her head. Thunder boomed above us, and the horse reared up again.

"Take him to that shelter," Crowe yelled, pointing at the medieval market, where some of the stalls were tented. The horse and I made our way through the field that was quickly turning to mud, and the shelter made us both feel calmer. I was beginning to feel cold, so I stood next to Quicksilver and put my arm around his neck. We watched as the rain smashed down into the ground and lightning scratched the sky, and I wondered where Izzy had gone.

The people and the wares were missing, but there was a table nearby that had a wooden box on it. I walked up to it and looked through its glass display lid. It reminded me of those cigar boxes in expensive lounges, but instead of fragrant Cubanos inside, rolled between the thighs of virgins, there was a satin cushion holding a dozen wands.

I remembered walking past this stall with Bron after I'd granted him a name. Kresnik. Shifter. Little did I know he'd be cursed to remain a bird forever. I touched the top of the case. He had looked at these wands with such longing, and he had been doing so well in his apprenticeship, I felt bad pulling him away. But what I had said to him was important and true. You don't just buy a wand. It doesn't work like that. But now I was in this upside-down world and I didn't know anything about the rules there. And I thought, what would be the harm in taking a wand for Bron?

Quicksilver snuffled and stomped his hooves, and the storm swirled around us. I levered open the lid and surveyed the spell sticks. They looked like typical flea-market knockoffs, and I doubted any of them held any real power. I chose a green one that would match the jade buttons of Bron's eyes. But as soon as I touched the wand a hand grabbed me from behind the table, and I jumped. When I looked up from the case I realized it had been an enchanted trap. The surroundings melted and peeled away like paint under a blowtorch, and soon I was no longer at the fair but deep in the Ever-Shade market.

"Got you," snarled a man, tightening his grip on my wrist.

"No!" I yelled, trying to get away. The air was just as I remembered it, thick with that invisible black mist that got right up your nostrils and coated your lungs with foul smoke.

"Caught red-handed just like the thief I've always known you are." His nails were digging into me as I pulled away from him.

I looked around for help. For Crowe, or Quicksilver, but only evil masks stared back. I looked at my captor. I had recognized his voice. But what was he doing here?

He moved his mask up, revealing his sneering face. My skin was painted cold with dread.

"Musubarin," I said.

"Jacquelyn Denna Knight."

"You put an enchantment on that case." Honestly, I wouldn't have expected such advanced magic from him. But we were, after all, in a parallel reality.

"A trick for a trick," he said, no doubt alluding to the conjuring spell I had caught him out with the last time we had seen each other. "This time, you won't get away so easily."

CHAPTER 15
THE DREAM DRINKER

Tilexon hauled me away from the market and forced me into the cabin of a nearby vehicle. When I noticed officer Tshabalala in the back seat, I felt relieved, remembering the kindness he had shown to the untouched woman who had slammed into their car. He didn't smile back. His eyes had the silver lenses of the possessed zombie army, and I screamed and flailed as he lunged at me. He held me down and pushed a white gauze cloth over my mouth. It had a sweet chemical smell. Chloroform.

I don't understand the rules here, I thought, as my consciousness leaked away. It felt as if the odds were forever stacked against me in this strange world, that the evil people could do whatever they desired. I had no perspective in this kingdom, no agency. I felt chilled thinking that this is how the whole Realm would be under the reign of the Silvanos. It was not a world I wanted to live in.

I considered fighting against the cold wet pad pressed up against my lips and nose, but I knew I didn't stand a chance. I didn't have the energy to lift my arms, never mind hand-to-hand combat with an officer who wore his biceps like Captain America. The sweetness seeped into me, cold turning warm, and my thoughts faded to a static screen, and then to a blip, and everything went dark and numb.

I WOKE up in a small gray cell. My head was pounding with the mothertrucker of all headaches, and my first thought was that Musubarin had finally managed to get me locked up in the Scorpion SubT cells. But I was wrong. There was a small window with bars on it, and when I looked outside I saw the overcast sky. I was high above the ground, in some sort of turret. It was surrounded by tall, straight trees. It reminded me of Darick's panic room, which, oddly, made me want to cry. The only decoration in the small, round room was a pattern etched into the concrete walls. I walked up to it and placed my palm on the grooves. Something about it felt familiar. I stepped back, trying to look at it properly, but all I saw were swirls and lines that swooped around each other. My skull ached, my eyeballs spiked with pain.

I felt in my pocket for Gizmo to see if he was okay, but it was empty.

Oh no, I thought. *No!* My heart raced and my stomach cramped with terror. Tilexon had taken Gizmo again, and this time I knew he wouldn't hesitate to kill him. I had to get out of that prison and find him before it was too late.

There was movement at the window, and a shuffling of feathers.

"Bron!" I said, my own loud voice making my temples blaze. He kwooked at me and nodded. "Can you get help? Crowe's around somewhere. So are Morgan and Darick."

The raven stared at me, then nodded and disappeared in a snap of black wings. Only the Void knew what kinds of nightmares Morgan and Darick were being put through. How many hoops would we have to jump through to get to the castle? I trusted Gizmo, but I worried that we were being sent on some kind of wild goose chase. Volcanic islands and fire-breathing Komodos and speedboats and palominos and battles with zombie witches in spooky forests. Acheron was keeping us occupied while he was putting his final touches to his New Dawn Throne. The problem was, there was nothing I could do about it. I didn't know the rules, or where the hell I was going. All I could do was focus on staying alive. It was infuriating knowing he was toying with us. He was preparing for his final *coup de grace* while I was just scrambling to survive.

"Sink or swim, baby," I said out loud, just so that I could hear something other than the claustrophobic closeness of the air around me. I tapped my pocket. I still had the Chaos Jar. So Acheron Baldassare would have to deal with me eventually.

I sat down on the screed floor and stared at the writing on the wall. As I looked at the curves and the slants, I recognized the pattern. Or, rather, I recognized the handwriting. Of course, the words were in Latin. Set out on the wall all around me was the fairy tale that Slyden Abarim engraved into his brother's skin. The Dream Drinker.

Oh, holy hex.

SaltySnap had not been exaggerating when she had said this evil parallel reality played on your fears. I had been so spooked by this children's story that I hadn't even opened the beautiful gold-embossed book that Blimaex had given me in thanks for saving him from Slyden's Contagious Magic. But I knew the story.

TWO RABBITS, one naughty, one nice, had always wanted someone to love them. They squabbled a great deal, but then they had to overcome their differences in order to save a girl wizard from a tower, who was being held there by a powerful older wizard so that he could drink her dreams, and in that way, steal her magical power. Because of this, his magic grew potent, almost to the point where he was indestructible, but the rabbits worked together to trick him and free the young girl, and she adopted them and cared for them for the rest of their lives, and they lived happily ever after.

Now, I was never the star pupil in the fae literature class at Copperfield, but I was guessing that the fairy tale could be applied in the following way: I was the wizard trapped in a tower and Musubarin was the evil wizard intent on stealing my magic. What I didn't know was how I was going to find a pair of rabbits to save me. I sat there on the floor and ran through the various plans of action in my head.

I could attempt to conjure up the rabbits. The problem with that was my conjuring magic was still being fed to Quicksilver, wherever he was, and I didn't think there'd be enough left over to create two extra creatures. Also, let's be honest, what were two little fluffy bunnies going to do to trick Tilexon? I didn't see it having a happy ending.

I could try to destroy the bars on the window, but then what? Plummet to my lonely death down below? I'd been there, done that, but this time Darick wasn't here to pull me back from the brink.

I pulled out my portal key, but before I tried it I knew it was a lost cause. It felt dead in my hands. There was no energy in it, no promise.

"Ianua sit," I said. As I had guessed, I remained where I was. I sighed and put it back in my pocket. I was getting really sick of men putting me in basements and panic rooms and towers that cut off my magic. Really, really sick of it. Anger boiled up inside me, and to add insult to injury, there was no magic that accompanied the fury. I felt like punching the walls, but I didn't want to hurt myself. I needed my hands in perfect working order so that I'd be ready for my battle with the Silvanos.

Then I heard something. Someone calling my name from outside, and I went to the small square window and peered out.

Standing on the carpet of grass below were my twin rescuer rabbits.

CHAPTER 16
VOLAS

Eafaris and Pepin Belore shouted and waved at me. Okay, so they weren't really rabbits, but they were definitely there to rescue me.

"Jax!" The twins shouted. "Jax!"

I wanted to ask them how they had found me, but then I saw Gizmo in Pip's arms. He must have escaped when Musubarin had grabbed me at EverShade. I was so relieved I felt like crying. I had so many questions for them, but there was no time for catching up. Knowing Tilexon, he'd be lurking somewhere close by. I was sure he'd love to lock the twins up, too. In fact, by now I was pretty sure that the Scorpion captain was on Acheron's payroll, and he'd probably be getting a generous sum for each of our heads.

It had always puzzled me that Musubarin was so intent on grabbing me. But then, of course, it all made sense. He had been appointed to captain the Scorpions by the Council, and the Council had been mesmerized by Acheron. Alif Farzad had been hired to spy on me, and Darick to assassinate me. The Silvano Clan had pulled out all the stops to bring me under their control. When Darick failed to kill me per their instructions, the plan changed: Darick was to be killed, and I was to be brought in alive.

They knew I had the Chaos Jar in my infinity pocket, and they knew how infinity pockets worked. Only the will of the owner could extract objects; they could not be stolen or forced out. They needed me because I had the final fragment, the last puzzle piece needed to complete the New Dawn.

The Belore twins stood below, and I was fifty feet up and behind bars. We needed to move quickly if we were to avoid Musubarin's greasy clutches.

"Eafy," I shouted. "Can you *rumpis* these bars?"

They may have been children, and mostly unskilled in their magic, but when they combined their power it became potent. I had seen them in action. Together—and with the help of their father's Dragon's Eye amulet—they had unleashed one of the most elegant Death Spells I had ever seen, destroying the murderous Morninglark Harp and taking out the evil vampire DeadWing. Suffice to say, novices or not, I was glad we were on the same team. The music still haunted my dreams.

Eafaris drew his hands up to his mouth to call out to me. "Too dangerous!"

Deodamnatus, I thought. He was probably right.

"How's your fire magic?" I yelled.

"What?"

"Ignem!" I shouted, and they nodded. Elemental Magic 101. If they could melt the bars, I'd be able to bend them. "Do you think it will reach this high?"

They chatted to each other and nodded.

"Stand back!" Pepin shouted.

I stood against the wall and felt the coolness of the cement. A blaze of blue fire appeared in the window. At first the bars seemed heat-resistant, and I wanted to kick something. As I watched they slowly turned from black to orange, to yellow, to white. When the blue fire retreated I pulled off my trench coat and used it to protect my hands as I bent the bars enough to fit my body through. The metal sizzled against the graphene, and I felt the heat on my palms, but there was no pain. I stuck my head through and gave them the thumbs-up, and they cheered.

I heard Ferra's voice in my head. *Good work, skunks.*

The next challenge was to get down from there without breaking every bone in my body.

"Any ideas?" I shouted.

Of course, they could have tried *Volas,* a levitation spell, but it was dangerous. I'd be too heavy for them to carry and the chances of them getting me down safely without dropping me were not good.

Pepin said something to her brother. I saw him nod. Then she looked down at her jeans and unbuckled her belt. She held it out in front of her and Eafaris started incanting a spell I couldn't hear. The belt grew longer and longer, until it was like a coil of rope. Having reached its full potential, it stopped growing, despite Eafy urging it on. The twins wouldn't have learnt this yet, but you can't stretch an object beyond its inherent potential.

"*Volas!*" shouted Pip, and threw the belt up towards me. I caught it and unraveled it outside the window. The belt was very long now, but not long enough for me to climb down, Rapunzel style. The kids looked up at me, frowning, not sure what to try next.

"I have an idea!" I shouted. I unclipped my crossbow.

I tied one end of the belt to the coolest bar, and tied the other end to an arrow head. I aimed the bow halfway down the closest tree and pulled the trigger. The bolt whooshed away from me and found the trunk of the tree, and slammed into it with a satisfying *thunk*. I tightened the belt from my side, pulled it taut, and climbed out through the bent bars. I threw my coat over the belt, grabbing hold of it on either side of the makeshift zip-line. I swallowed hard, hesitating for a second before leaping out, my heartbeat crashing in my ears. It wouldn't be the first time I had jumped out of a window, and I hoped it wouldn't be the last.

I took a breath and stepped off the ledge, and immediately went rushing down. I had to let go at the right moment. Too soon, and I'd be too high up. Too late, and I'd smash my skeleton to smithereens on the trunk of the tree. I zipped down fast—too fast—and tried to keep my nerve despite the speed and the fact that I seemed to have left my stomach behind in the tower. As I got halfway—still too high up to survive the fall—the belt snapped and whipped backwards, and I plummeted.

The twins were ready. They both pushed their arms out toward me and shouted *"Volas! Volas! Volas!"*

While their quick-thinking magic wasn't strong enough to hold my full weight, they slowed my descent. I landed with a bang, and the air was knocked out of my lungs. I dragged in a couple of breaths, then inspected my body. I was uninjured.

The twins raced up to me with pale faces.

"Are you okay?"

"Is anything broken?"

"Is anything *not* broken?"

I looked up at them, shielding my eyes from the glare of the overcast sky. "Some good spell-slinging there, skunks," I wheezed, and they smiled.

CHAPTER 17

RAT FANG

"Thank you for coming to rescue me," I said, shaking my coat back on as we hurried away from the tower. I was certain Musubarin would be close on our heels, and I wasn't in the mood for another chloroform cocktail.

Gizmo leapt from Pip's arms into mine, and scurried into my pocket.

"Thank Gizmo," said Eafaris. "We would never have been able to find you without him."

Where had they come from, I wondered. How did they find Salty's gateway? Had they heard the call of the portal? If they had heard it, who else had?

"Where's Ferra?" I asked, and the twins' faces dropped. "We haven't seen her since we left the fox den."

My heart swelled, thinking of my dwarf surrogate mother. "Don't worry," I said, ruffling their hair. "We'll find her."

I felt uncomfortable having the twins in the New Dawn Kingdom. Everything was so unpredictable and dangerous. The children had already lost their parents. If anything happened to them, I'd find it very difficult to live with.

We kept walking, and the landscape soon turned from a meadow painted white gold by the obfuscated sunset, to darkness swirling with menace. I realized that the kingdom didn't have a predictable set of day and night, and the weather did as it pleased. It could be storming in the afternoon at the medieval fair, as it had done, and be a fresh sunny morning just a few fields away. It could flash through day and night a hundred times in twenty-four hours, and play with every spectrum of weather.

We slowed down in the dim light. It was difficult to see until we'd lit our wands, and the soil was soft. We came to a wrought iron gate on which hung a destroyed padlock.

Uh-oh, I thought. I recognized the gate, and the lock that I had previously melted. I held my wand up and read the sign above.

OBSIDIAN HILL CEMETERY

"Oh..." I said, and the twins both blinked at me, their eyes mirroring the gloom that surrounded us.

"What?" they both said at the same time.

"I don't think we should go in there," I said.

"But there's nowhere else to go," said Pepin, frowning. It was true. There was nothing else around us. The cemetery was the only way forward. I looked around, desperate to find a way around, but there was nothing. Just the giant iron gate and what lay beyond.

This wasn't real life. This wasn't a *Choose Your Own Adventure* book where we could skip to page 89. This was Acheron's lair, and he was going to make this as painful for us as he could.

Deodamnatus, I swore under my breath. He may think he was breaking me down with all this. That was probably his plan. But it was actually making me feel stronger. It was making me angry, and with the anger, my resolve strengthened. I had feared the Silvanos before, but now a new emotion was blooming in my chest, one I knew I could use to fight Acheron. This pain and fear he was dishing out to me would only make my magic stronger.

I've known since my days on the city streets that pain augmented my power. On the days I was homesick and missing my parents I could feel the magic bubbling away inside me. Over time, I learned how to harness the pain and transform it into power. It's called Blood Magic and it is my superpower.

Dark arts practitioners use Blood Magic to harm others, and the pain they cause is then fed into the loop to fuel their spells. They are able to build it and build it until their magic is far stronger than their natural ability, which causes havoc with all kinds of delicately balanced magical systems. Slyden Abarim used his brother's pain to augment his magic, while he sold his Magus—and his soul—to Acheron. I don't even want to know how much Magus Acheron had banked over the decades, but it was enough to create this mad, bad, dangerous world. I knew it was up to me to take it all away from him.

I took a deep breath and opened the gate. The hinges creaked, and it felt like the sound traveled into my body and into my bones. I shivered. I didn't want to take the children into the cemetery, but I didn't have a choice. We picked our way carefully over rocks and decaying branches. We reached the tombstones, which looked like dragons' teeth planted in the ground. With every step I felt more dread, until I was sick to my stomach. I held onto a gravestone and put my hand to my chest. Bile rushed into my mouth. I was afraid to spit it out; afraid that my body would think that was a green light to vomit.

"What is it?" asked Pip. "You don't look very well."

"Are you ill?" asked Eafy.

How could I not feel ill, when the last time I was here was a nightmare of giant suffocating spiderwebs and the rat-fang shredded corpse of their beloved father? I closed my eyes and tried to swallow my anxiety. I didn't want the kids any more traumatized than they already were.

"Get your wands out," I said, wiping my lips with the back of my hand. They frowned at me. Their wands were out. They were lighting the way.

"Get ready to use them," I said. "And be careful. Be very careful."

The soil was, as last time, too soft for comfort, and it made me wonder how many wizards' bodies were buried there. I heard the same hooting and howling as before, and I prayed that nothing would attack us. I wondered where Bron was, and Morgan, Darick, Quicksilver. It felt so isolated there on Obsidian Hill, as if we were the only humans for miles.

Silently we traipsed through the graveyard, shoes sinking into the humus and leafmold. Every now and then one of us tripped and found our footing again, and gestured to the others that we were okay. The unengraved tombstones were a constant reminder of how quickly the Reaper could snatch you; how quickly you'd be forgotten. Dust to dust. Blank slate to blank slate. I knew as well as anyone how quickly a flame could be snuffed out. We stumbled on.

CHAPTER 18
DEAD HOLOGRAM

Pepin cried out. I thought she had fallen, but when I looked at her face there was wonder there. I turned to see what she had spotted and my blood ran cold.

"Dad!" she cried, and she started to run to him.

A man sat on a small bentwood bench that had magically surfaced from the dread dark that surrounded us.

"No!" I shouted. "That's not your father!" I desperately looked at Eafaris for backup, but his face was lit up, too. Ametrix Belore stood up, his face glowing, his arms outstretched.

"It's a trap!" I shouted, but the children could not hear. Pepin ran straight into the specter's arms, and he hugged her to him, only letting go to welcome Eafaris with his other arm.

I clutched my wand, ready to fight, ready to protect the twins.

"Leave them alone," I said, and Ametrix looked at me, his face blank.

"Who are you?" he asked.

"The wizard who's going to kick your ass if you don't leave those kids alone."

"Jax! Don't!" said Pip, who had tears streaming down her face. "Can't you see? It's Dad!"

"No," I said, shaking my head. "This isn't real. None of this is real."

"I don't care!" she shouted. Eafaris started crying, too. I heard the howling in the distance again. I could feel the danger lurking in the dark. I wanted to get out of there.

The children were sobbing, and my eyes pricked with tears, too. It was so close to home. My heart swelled and ached for them, and for myself.

"We have to go," I said.

"I'm staying," said Pepin.

Eafaris nodded. "Me, too."

"You can't stay here," I said.

This realm wants to eat you, I thought. *It wants to swallow you up and then you'll just be a blip in the Void.* But I knew that sounded crazy, so instead I said, "We need to stop the people who did this to your family."

There was a sound behind me, someone walking, shoes

crunching on dead leaves. I whirled around. It was Francis Belore, and she was carrying the Morninglark Harp.

"Mom!" the twins shouted together, and they ran to her, almost knocking her off her feet. She had the same blank expression as Ametrix. She held the harp in one hand and embraced the children with the other. The kids were hiccupping and wiping their faces. Ametrix stood up and joined his family, and they stood there, together, the four of them.

"I have a song to play for you," said Francis.

"No!" I said, holding my wand out at her, but the children stood between us. "Cover your ears!"

Francis began to strum the instrument, and the wooden carvings on the side began to dance.

"Cover your ears!" I shouted again, but it was too late. The twins also had those scary blank expressions. Their relief was gone, as was their sorrow. Only pale white masks remained.

AMETRIX AND FRANCIS began to walk away, and the children followed them in a somnolent stumble through the cemetery.

"No!" I shouted again. I couldn't let them go. I raced after the twins, pulling them back, but it was as if their bodies were magnetized; their skulls empty.

"Stop!" I said to Francis, but the music coming from the harp was hypnotic and I had to cover my ears to stop it from cascading into my brain like it had before.

She turned around. "Come with us," she said, and my hips began to sway in her direction.

"Fiat fulgur!" I shouted, and a blue current barreled out of my wand and speared Francis in the heart, narrowly missing Pip's head. But nothing happened. Francis just smiled an empty smile and began to turn to walk away again.

"Fiat fulgur!" This time I aimed at the harp, but it was also resistant to my attack.

I didn't understand. I danced up to her and tried to take the harp away, but my hand just fell through her. She was a dead hologram, and yet the twins were able to hold her hand.

I couldn't let the harp music into my head. Already I felt the pull of the tune, deep inside me, as if it were speaking to the core of my body. I stopped trying to sling spells at them and covered my ears, instead. I sang loudly to myself to block out the magical melody.

It made me remember the time I had been belting out a song in my goblin-sized shower at home, only to realize afterwards that Darick had been there all along. When he passed me a towel I was mortified. No wonder we haven't sealed the deal yet; he's probably afraid for the wellbeing of his ears.

The Belore family continued to walk away from me, stumbling over the uneven, soft soil, and dodging the dragon's teeth. I didn't know what to do. Death was literally marching the children away from me and I was out of ideas.

There was a growling. A deep, dangerous sound that cut through the harp's music and my own abysmal singing. I flinched and clutched my wand again, ready to defend myself and the children.

A wolf leapt out in the Belores' path. He snarled at them, showing all his sharp teeth and black gums.

I ran through some spells in my head, but the sudden appearance of the wolf had shocked me into a kind of brain malfunction and I came up empty.

"Away!" I shouted at him, moving closer. I lit the end of my wand with a proper flame and waved it at him. "Away!"

I wanted to get between the wolf and the children, to protect them, but he had other ideas. Before I could do anything, he leapt at Pepin, snarling and growling, and knocked her to the ground.

CHAPTER 19

WHEN YOU'RE DEAD YOU SEE EVERYTHING

S hock almost knocked me down. I held tightly to my wand and screamed, *"Fiat fulgur!"*

A lightning bolt travelled toward the wolf but he deftly ducked it. He was standing with his paws on Pepin's chest, who had lost consciousness, and he looked up at me. There was something about his eyes. It was dark, but there was something—

I got ready to sling another current but then the wolf spoke.

"Jacquelyn Denna Knight," he growled. "We've been waiting for you."

Ametrix and Francis had disappeared. Eafaris blinked a few times and then looked at me, his face stamped with confusion.

"Jax?" he said, in a voice that sounded younger than his years. "What happened?" Then he looked at the wolf. "Rusty? Is that you?"

The werewolf transformed before us into the human form we knew so well. He still wore his Copperfield Institute security guard uniform.

"Rusty!" I said. I wanted to hug him but just moments ago I'd seen his snarl and I still had adrenaline pumping through my body. "What are you doing here?"

He looked at me, flashing his canines in the moonlight. "You have no idea what you've done."

My blood ran cold. "Me? What? What do you mean?"

"You fractured the Void," he said, leaning to pick up Pepin and hoisting her over his shoulder.

Oh. That.

"I didn't mean to," I said. "I thought destroying the Chaos Jar would be the only way to stop Acheron from taking over the Realm."

"There is no way to stop Acheron," he growled.

"Don't say that."

"I've seen the future," said Rusty. "When you're dead, you see everything."

"Do you?"

I thought you saw nothing. I thought that was the whole point of being dead; resting.

"Rest is for the untouched," he said.

"Can you explain to me how this works? I don't understand."

"We don't have time."

"I need to know why I could use magic on the Komodo dragons and Ophelia, but not on Ametrix and Francis. I need to know how you got here, even though I saw your dead body at Copperfield."

"The answer is in your pocket," he said.

"It's not the greatest time to be enigmatic," I said. "I have a Realm to save."

"The answer is literally in your pocket," he said.

"The Chaos Jar?"

Seriously, you break one little jar and no one ever lets you forget it.

"When you fractured the Void you allowed spirits to roam freely. You allowed Wild Magic to leak into the Realm."

"But we're not in the Realm," I said. "This is the New Dawn Kingdom. This is *Acheron's* pocket."

"Oh, it's all the Realm," he said, voice gruff. "Everything is the Realm. That's why, if you die here, you die there."

He may as well have been speaking in Orcish for all I understood.

"You said you've seen the future," I said. "You said the Silvanos cannot be defeated." I looked around the cemetery. "Is this what life will be like now?"

"You know the answer to that," said Rusty.

"I don't!" I yelled. "I don't know anything!"

"I'm just a werewolf," he said, shrugging. Pepin's body hung limply over his shoulder. "I'm just a rusty werewolf. You're the one with the Jar in your pocket."

WE LOPED out of Obsidian Hill Cemetery, and I made sure to not step into any giant spiderwebs. I had almost been killed by a web last time, and I had the feeling the hungry spider was around, waiting for her prodigal wizard dinner. My tired and traumatized brain imagined the twins' dead parents transforming into the spiders, and luring the children away to spin them into silken spring rolls.

I shivered, and kept walking. I felt as if I had been walking for days. Maybe I *had* been walking for days. I had passed through so many dimensions my thoughts and memories were tangled up. I didn't let my anxiety get the best of me. I focused on my top priority. I needed to save my parents and kill Acheron. Rusty said it was impossible, but he had to be wrong.

He said he saw the future, but perhaps it was just a possible future. With Wild Magic zinging around and realms leaking into realms, who knew what was real and what was not? Did the concept of "real" even exist anymore? I hoped so. I still fantasized about a life that was kind of back to normal.

Getting home to Ghost and freshly laundered pajamas.

Gizmo's Barbie Dreamhouse.

Dinners at The Copper Cog & Ale.

Drinks with Morgan at an overpriced cocktail bar.

Figuring out Darick.

Fighting evil—and winning.

I hadn't known how good I'd had it. It all seemed a lifetime ago, but I would fight for it. I would fight for it all.

RUSTY TOOK THE LEAD, and Eafy and I fell behind. I sensed he wanted to talk.

"I had a dream," he said. "I had a dream that I saw my parents again."

"Oh?" I wasn't sure how much I should say.

"They were showing me the way."

"The way?"

"The way to be with them. Forever."

"You mean ... to die?"

He shook his head and raked his fingers through his hair. "I don't know."

"Did you want to die?"

He stopped and looked at me. "I don't know. Yes. At the time."

"I'd prefer it if you kept breathing," I said, punching him on the shoulder.

"Okay," he said.

"I need you in my corner," I said. "I need you. Your sister needs you. We're up against the most evil vampire in the history of ever. We're going to need all the help we can get."

Something in his eyes was different, as if the holograms had touched his psyche in a way I didn't like. As if they had made death seem like a rather attractive option.

I grabbed his arm. "Okay?"

He nodded. "Okay."

We started to walk again, in the werewolf's footsteps, but I felt uneasy. It seemed to me that the ever-shifting terrain didn't just apply to the landscape in Acheron's kingdom, but to minds, too, and this new knowledge made me feel very cold inside.

CHAPTER 20
COALS AND SNOW

"Where are we going?" I asked Rusty. "Is this the way to the castle?"

The air was crisp now, and his panting breath came out in plumes of white.

"Somewhere safe," he said.

"Safe?" I said. "Not here. Nowhere here is safe."

"True," he said. "But it's the safest place I know."

WHEN WE ARRIVED at the Copperfield Institute, it was snowing, and the sun was yet again on the rise. My body was exhausted, and Eafy was practically asleep on his feet. Perhaps a quick rest would do us good. I needed to be in top form when I finally saw Acheron. Rusty took us straight to Directress Copperfield's house. I tried not to look too closely at the ruins that used to be the best magical academy on the continent. The white snow was in sharp contrast to the burnt hull of what used to be the school hall. The fields were black, the buildings razed, as if the Hammerskins had driven that tank over every building they had found. Even the canteen and the rooms they had annexed for the civil war were destroyed. There was nothing left.

The Directress's house loomed in the distance. It was the only building that had survived—due, I was sure, to the strength of the protection spell she had placed on it. We trudged across the coals and snow, and I pulled my coat tighter against the cold. I watched as snowflakes fell on Rusty's athletic shoulders and melted against his tufted pelt.

The snow made me feel emotional. I wasn't sure why. Or maybe it was just being there and seeing the terrible waste all around. Where would touched children go, now? Who would take in the orphans? Where would they learn the difference between dark and light? How would they learn how to focus their power?

Nowhere was the answer, and it was all part of the Silvanos' plan. I hated them so much in that moment, I could feel the anger racing in my veins.

"Hey," said Rusty, who had seen me stop.

I looked up at him, bristling with all the emotion I was feeling.

"Are you coming?"

"I'll be with you in a sec. I just need to walk around a bit."

"We've been walking for hours," said Rusty. "Why don't you come in with us? We can grab a glass of water."

A glass of water did sound good.

"I'll be right behind you," I said.

Rusty nodded, and took the children into the house. Pepin had not yet gained consciousness, and I was worried about her. I was worried that the holograms had taken more from her than she had to give.

I walked in the pure, bright snow, enjoying the novelty of it, and the crushing sound it made under my boots. The jacarandas had lost their purple blooms, but the white dusting on their branches looked pretty. I preferred to gaze at them rather than the classrooms, which had been burnt to the ground and were now vulnerable to the elements.

How much of this was my fault? I wondered. The fracture in the Jar had spilt chaos in every direction, and I couldn't tell what was caused by Wild Magic and what the Silvanos had corrupted. The last twenty-four hours felt like a Dali dream. Except that our clocks weren't melting; they were ticking away to our doom.

THE SNOWFALL BECAME HEAVIER, and the sky was a light, watercolor gray. I was drawn to the quad. I knew I'd find the bronze statue of Minerva toppled; I had seen that the last time I had visited Copperfield, to collect the twins for Ferra. It bothered me. It seemed to epitomize the disrespect the Hammerskins showed for the magical institutions I revered. I knew that most of the Neo-Nazi orcs had been dispatched to Halloween Heaven, courtesy of a mass-murdering pickle face who I was beginning to feel a growing affection for, despite her pronounced halitosis and clear psychopathic tendencies. And I knew this wasn't real—that none of it was real and all of it was real—but that was pretty normal for me nowadays. When you're hired by vain, sneaky elves with Dorian Gray complexes and women who are haunted by their dead husbands, and assassins repeatedly save your life, you get to know your new normal—and none of it is "normal."

The wind picked up, making the snow flurry around me. I tightened my coat again.

"Nano. Scarf."

My nano leapt out of my pocket and wound itself around my neck, offering instant protection from the icy wind that had begun to howl around me.

I saw the statue of Minerva lying on the frozen ground, covered in snow, and I padded over to it. The quad was silent; the only sound was the crunching of my boots on the icy powder. I rubbed the snow away from her face, which was freezing to the touch. I scraped it away from her hip, where I had once found her stray owl, and was delighted to see the bird again. It was the same owl as I had seen that day as a teenager, but then, kneeling in the snow, I saw it in startling detail. His eyes were wide and beautiful. Old and wise, but alert at the same time. Each individual feather was visible, and his beak looked powerful and sharp, a lethal weapon that could snap a lemming's neck just by virtue of its existence. I would have gazed for longer, but the blizzard became so powerful that I was forced to hunch down and lean on the statue for support. The sky darkened, and I realized that I wasn't dressed for this kind of arctic weather. A nano scarf was one thing, but I could already feel my feet freezing and my ankles stiffening as the cold traveled up my body. I'd need to get inside with the rest of them if I didn't want to turn into a wizard popsicle.

My right hand—the one that was touching the owl—began to feel warm and I frowned and looked down at it. The snow on Minerva's cloak was melting. The owl seemed to be staring at me.

I was freezing. My body was numb. I felt that if I didn't break for the house right then I'd lose a couple of limbs to frostbite. I took my hand off Minerva's owl, and it immediately froze up again. I put it back, touching the owl's head, and it defrosted again, leaking snowbroth to the ground around it. Any flakes falling on it immediately melted away. I pushed harder, wondering what would happen, and as I increased the pressure I found myself falling forward and into the cloak. I was tumbling through some kind of portal at such a speed it took my breath away.

No! I thought. *I couldn't leave the twins.* But I didn't have a choice. I was hurtling through a gateway I'd never seen before and there was no turning back.

CHAPTER 21
HOT SOUR STINK

I hit the ground hard, sending a shooting pain through my knees. My palms smacked the concrete, and I just managed to stop my skull from hitting the pavers. I didn't even look up at first, just stayed on my hands and knees, breathing to get through the pain. Slowly, it faded, and I was able to begin to take in the details around me. It was a grimy city pavement, and the shoes that marched past me were not contemporary; I guessed at 1980s or 90s. When I lifted my head, I saw that the clothes matched the shoes. I was on a busy city sidewalk. Or what a busy city sidewalk would have looked like twenty years ago.

I stood up and dusted my stinging palms, my aching knees. That's when I noticed the size of my hands. They were small and tender, and my fingernails were edged in dirt.

And I was short. Really short. The adults towered above me. I touched my face and looked down at my body. I was a child.

But not just any child. My clothes were grubby and I could smell the hot, sour stink of the street on my skin; the odor I had come to know so well when I was a Feral. A woman carrying shopping bags bumped into me and kept walking without apologizing. Her message was clear. I did not belong there. People like her thought that street urchins should be neither seen nor heard. In the old days I would have pick-pocketed something from her, but as it was, I stood there in a daze. What was I doing there?

I started to walk, recognizing the street. I knew it well. The Ferals and I had an abandoned building two blocks up that kept us warm at night if we managed to stuff the cracks with enough balled up newspaper and cover the floor with the cardboard from broken boxes nicked from the Portuguese grocer on Simmonds. With enough children crammed into the small room we were able to keep it warm with our body heat, but lice were always a problem. The itchiness would drive us crazy and we'd beg the old man outside the taxi rank to shave our heads for us with his oiled clippers, but he'd shoo us away. He couldn't risk spreading the parasite to his customers. The lice and bed bugs and fleas and cockroaches weren't the only things to take up residence in our squat. There were also city rats, which were as big as Elf Estate chihuahuas. They'd come in at night while we were sleeping and squeak and sniff around us, looking for the crumbs we'd invariably have in our pockets, or crusts of bread wrapped up in threadbare handkerchiefs: our breakfasts for the next day. We soon learned not to keep any food in our clothes, no matter how much we craved it. I could go a whole day without eating if I knew I had food in my pocket. I slept better, too, knowing I'd have something to eat in the morning. But after those rats sought us out we became easy pickings for them, and I decided I'd rather wake up hungry than with a cat-sized rat on my chest. We'd turn away new kids that were too young. Before the rats had arrived, we'd welcome anyone: the more bodies, the more body heat. But the rats would bite the smaller children, and it was nightmarish waking up to a child screaming in the night. Bloodcurdling; eyes wide with terror. We decided not to let them stay at all. It seemed cruel to turn them away but we were probably doing them a favor. A small part of me was relieved to make them go. They looked so vulnerable to me; I seemed positively grown up at nine years old compared to their tender little faces. I found it difficult to deal with seeing them adrift in the city. Where were their parents? Did no one care?

We'll find a better place to live, we'd daydream out loud, our small bodies all smooshed together to stay warm. Then we'd be able to look after the babies. We'd find a better place and then we'd no longer have to turn them away.

As soon as winter's over we'll find a better place. A cleaner place. A place that didn't want to feed on us. As if we had anything to give.

SOMEONE ELSE BUMPED INTO ME, snapping me out of my memories. I saw a shop sign I recognized, and then another. A discount sneaker store, a bank, a pawn shop. I knew this strip well. I kept walking and I was bombarded with more memories. That was the shop that always sprayed fake snow on its display window for Christmas. That was the corner that Lebogang was bumped by a car. I stopped outside a convenience store boasting Dunhill filters for R5. We weren't allowed in that shop. The owner and cashier both knew how proficient we were at sneaking things off their shelves.

Someone whistled in the distance, and it made me look up. There was hooting and yelling up the road. Some small commotion; a driver shouting at a pedestrian. Then the car drove away, and that's when I saw Mister Hot Dog.

CHAPTER 22
MISTER HOT DOG

I was nine years old and living on the gray streets in downtown Jo'burg. I looked down again at my palm and saw the twenty-rand note. I remembered that I had just used my burgeoning magic to slip the money out of a passerby's cream linen pocket, and I was dreaming of the bag of hot chips I was going to buy with it. I was too hungry to feel guilty. When I joined the small gang of street kids I was a traumatized little girl, lost in every way. They took me in and taught me their special brand of magic: quick and dirty spells that you could sneak into almost any scenario without being caught. The money in my hand was proof that I could look after myself. It made me feel clever and strong and independent, and less broken. It was everything to me.

Mister Hot Dog would give us his expired food if we didn't hang around and bother his paying customers. There was a funny painting of a Vienna sausage man wearing a long bun on his shop-front, with a squiggle of tomato sauce running down his body. Mister Hot Dog was having a slow week and didn't have *leftovers for us, so a couple of us hadn't eaten in a while. Those days on the streets were when I got to know my inner werewolf.*

I clutched the cash in my small hand—black-nailed and grubby —and set my sight on Mister Hot Dog's greasy service window. It was one of my favorite places in the world, especially in the cold of winter. Hot kitchen air would billow out and keep me warm in quick, stolen snatches of walking past. No hanging around, though, to breathe in the old-sunflower-oil deep-fryer smell, or the aroma of swollen frankfurters in their warming drawer. No loitering to defrost blue fingers, or we wouldn't get our scraps. But this time I had money, and I'd be able to stand in the short queue and feel the steam on my face and my icy hands as I waited with the other paying customers. I knew Mister Hot Dog would stuff my packet with as many extra chips as it could handle without splitting down the sides, so I'd be able to share them with my fellow Ferals without feeling much anguish. I thought of the spice and the vinegar, and I began to salivate.

I MUST HAVE BEEN ten steps away from the food when the thug grabbed me. He was wearing some kind of invisibility enchantment so when he picked me up by the scruff of my neck I felt like I was flying. I kicked and screamed and he slammed his palm over my mouth so hard that my teeth cut my lip. I could taste the blood.

So much blood in my memories; sometimes I feel as if my whole life has been stained by blood. Crimson-tinted glasses.

I kept writhing and kicking, and screaming into his hot, salty palm, which was as big as my face. He growled at me to keep quiet, but I had other plans.

"Monstras!" I shouted. It was a reveal-spell that the Ferals had taught me. The invisibility enchantment rustled and fell off the man like a slippery satin scarf. I looked at his wide, determined face, and screamed right into it, blood spraying his cheek.

"Help!" I yelled. "Help!" but my words were muffled. I already knew from experience that people didn't stop to help children in rags, even when they were in trouble. If I had been wearing a pretty dress, and my hair was washed and braided, my skin scrubbed, maybe strangers would have stopped the man, demanded he let me go, but I was not a cherished child. Not anymore.

The twenty-rand note fluttered to the ground.

A bronze-colored SUV pulled up, and the passenger door was flung open. The kidnapper hurled me inside as if I were a rugby ball, then slid in and slammed the door.

"Go!" he instructed the driver behind the smoked-glass screen. He looked around, checking for potential witnesses, or anyone who may have wanted to stop us—

CHAPTER 23
A LITTLE BROWN BIRD

The memory was so vivid, so pungent I could still smell the abductor's palm over my mouth. My heart was racing and I had to tell myself I was okay, everything was okay. I swallowed hard and clutched the money in my tender-skinned hand, which felt leathery and damp. I was still standing on the pavement. No one had taken me ... yet.

I forced myself to gain perspective. The abduction had been traumatic, and I hated the way the man had just grabbed me off the street like that, as if I were a stray dog. But at the end of it all he had actually rescued me from a great deal of suffering. The urchin life had taught me a lot and toughened me up—there were life lessons learned in those years that I wouldn't have been able to get anywhere else—but living there any longer would have blunted my soul.

There are some things you never forget.

The abductor, despite his rough manner, delivered me to the Copperfield Institute. It had been a difficult adjustment but it had probably saved my life. I learned quick and dirty magic from the Ferals, and I learned elemental magic from the professors at Copperfield. It set me up to be able to make a living from my magic—not like those trust-fund wizards who study their whole lives away, obsessed with theory and doctorates—and although I've never felt particularly accomplished or successful, it does make me proud to think that I have made a life for myself.

Granted, my haunted apartment is the size of postage stamp, and my refrigerator is so bare it would fit in well on a nudist beach, but I have a roof over my head and people to love. At least ... I *had* a roof over my head ... who knows what my place looked like now, or if it was still standing at all. It may have been bombed by the last of the Hammerskins, or eaten by the jungle plant. Thinking about my home made me wonder where Ghost was, and how one would go about relocating a specter.

I looked down at my hand again, gripping the note so tightly, and I eased my fingers, one by one, until it was free. A breeze snatched it from my palm, and it went skipping away from me. A little brown bird. I watched it until it flew out of sight.

The traffic beside me was noisy, but the sound was muffled. Pedestrians walked past, but I hardly took them in. I was focused on Mister Hot Dog. I walked toward the painting of the Vienna with its playful squiggle of red sauce.

• • •

OF COURSE, as soon as I got to within a couple of meters of the food vendor, I was snatched off the street. He slammed his hand over my mouth so that I couldn't scream, and I felt the familiar slicing of lip as my teeth cut into them. He was invisible, as he was in my memory, and in all my subsequent dreams. And, as always, I stripped him of the enchantment by using the reveal spell the Ferals had taught me.

"*Monstras!*"

This time I shouldn't fight, I thought. I knew where he was taking me. I swallowed the blood and tried to unclamp my jaw, tried to keep my little feet from kicking him in the shins, but I had little control over that adrenaline-swamped child's body. I didn't want to fight him; knew I shouldn't fight him, but my legs had other ideas. The vehicle glided to a stop. The bronze-colored SUV I knew so well. The door opened, and the man was about to sling me inside.

Then something odd happened.

A SMALL BOY APPEARED, blocking the man's way. He was slightly older than I was, had white-blond hair, a handsome face, and the kind of killer cheekbones I'd recognize anywhere. I'd never seen him without a cape on before, and he looked like a normal kid. He looked up at my abductor with a snarl on his face.

"Leave her alone," he demanded.

"Get out of my way, kid," barked the man.

"I'm warning you," the boy said. "Put her down right now or you'll be sorry."

I had the feeling the man wanted to boot the boy out of the way, but perhaps his compassion forbade it. He wasn't an ogre, after all. He was just doing his job.

He kept advancing toward the car with me struggling in his arms, and the blond boy's eyes glinted with fury. He rose up in the air and smashed his hand into the man's neck, causing him to drop me onto the hard, hot pavement. The boy dropped at the same time, and grabbed the invisibility cloak that was lying there. We huddled together as he quickly covered us with it, and we both disappeared.

CHAPTER 24
A FATE WORSE THAN DEATH

As we crouched under the invisibility cloak I looked into the boy's intense eyes that mirrored my own. It was only for a moment, then he pulled it off again, and we were no longer on that Jo'burg city street, and we were no longer children.

Mist swirled all around us, and there was a chill in the air. Tall dark conifers, black-needled, and a dark gray sky. I pulled my coat tighter and buttoned my collar. I could feel that we were close to the nexus of the Silvano pocket realm, except that from what I had seen so far, it was no "pocket." The New Dawn Kingdom was huge and sprawling and it seemed infinite and infinitely dangerous. The castle loomed in the distance, as huge and menacing as I had expected it to be. My cheeks and fingers were cold.

The blond man never took his eyes off me. He was wearing his teal-lined cape.

"Lysander," I said.

"I've always regretted that," he said.

"Regretted what?"

"Not saving you that day. Letting them take you away."

"What?"

"I should have taken you before they did."

My head was spinning. "You knew me when I was nine years old?"

"I've always known you," he said.

I couldn't make sense of that. "I didn't need saving. They took me to the Copperfield Institute and it was the best thing that could have happened to me."

"No," he said. "You don't know that."

A bolt of lightning flashed across the sky, which was turning darker with every beat of my heart.

"What was the alternative?" I asked. "Freezing on the inner city streets? Starving to death?"

"You're shrewd. Crafty. Cunning. You would have survived. Besides, I could have taken you to—"

"Oh, I understand now," I said. "You didn't want Copperfield to kidnap me but you would have had no problem doing it yourself."

He shook his head. "Jax. There's so much you don't understand."

"Ah," I said, acting amused. I was not. "That old chestnut."

Fury burned in my chest. I was so damn sick and tired of being told that I didn't know the truth, that I didn't see the whole picture, that I didn't understand.

"We kept the truth from you to protect you," he said. "It was the only way to keep you out of danger."

"Who the *faex* is *we*?"

"If I had told you the truth you would have sought out Acheron."

"Ah, well," I said. "Guess what? I'm here now."

"I tried to keep you away."

Is that why he set that trap to get me arrested at the Crystal Clink? I can't really hold that against him. He was trying to keep me away from a ferry he knew would explode. Still, there's plenty I could hold against him.

The thought that had been pressing in on me, demanding to be addressed, blurted out of my mouth.

"You killed those women!" I shouted.

Lysander didn't deny that he was the V-Cult killer. "I was following orders."

"Spineless bastard."

"It was them or you," he muttered, looking down.

"What?"

"It was them or you, Jax. Acheron wanted you dead. I came up with plan to stall him."

"Killing a dozen innocent women?" I spluttered. "What kind of plan is that?"

"They were necessary sacrifices to keep you alive."

This knowledge hit me hard, as if Lysander had punched me in the stomach. So many women killed in cold blood to spare my life. The guilt seeped into me. I felt their collective presence. They appeared as gray ghosts standing behind me. First there were two, then six, then they all stood there, staring at Lysander with empty eyes. Last to appear was Liz Durison, who stood right next to me, and I could feel the anger radiating off her in cold waves.

"Their deaths—" said Lysander.

"Their *murders*," I corrected.

"They distracted you from finding the elemental fragments for long enough for the Silvanos to finish creating the New Dawn Kingdom. And, when Acheron demanded you be brought in, the bodies served as a trail of breadcrumbs to lead you here."

Dread coursed through me. So much for the element of surprise. "Acheron wants me here?"

"At the beginning, Acheron had you spied on through the Council he corrupted. He knew you posed a threat. When he had seen enough, he gave the order for the Council to take you out, but—"

"But the Council assassin failed."

"Yes. As did DeadWing. Acheron lost patience and said he'd do it himself, but I told him you'd be more valuable to him alive. He knew I was right. When Demetrius couldn't bring you in, I was tasked with the job."

The ghosts standing around me were getting restless. As one, they let out a low moan and their mouths were black holes. Liz Durison was trembling and her groan reverberated inside me.

I TRIED to step past him, and he said the same thing again. "I tried to keep you away."

"Well, it didn't work. You can step aside, now."

"You can't, Jax. You can't go to the castle."

I unclipped my wand, and Lysander's face paled at the sight of it.

"I can and I will, so I would advise you to step out of the way."

More lightning lit up the sky.

"I'm not going to let you go in there, Jax."

I tried to push past him, but he grabbed my forearm.

"Let me go," I said. "Let me go!"

I tried to wrench my arm away from him but he didn't relinquish his grip. As always, when we touched, there was a current flowing between us. A connection so deep and intense that I didn't understand it. There was no romance in it—I practically hated the guy, and he scared me—but there was a feeling between us that was unshakeable. What did he know?

Don't get distracted, I told myself. I was trying to ignore the emotions welling up but it didn't work. The wave threatened to engulf me, and something in me gave way beneath it.

"Leave me alone!" I screamed, battering his chest with my free fist. I lost control of my emotions and felt my magic threatening to leak out of me.

He pulled me close. "I'll let you go. Listen to me! I'll let you go, but I won't let you go in there."

I pushed away from him, and he finally lost his hold on me. I wiped my mouth and the back of my hand came away red. My lip was still bleeding from where my teeth had cut into it.

"You think I take directions from a *vampire*?" I said. I injected as much vitriol as I could in the word "*vampire*." I knew it would hurt him, but I didn't know why. Maybe he had seen my bedpost, with its hundreds of notches of vampire kills. My magic was flowing freely through my body and I struggled to keep it under control. I needed to be careful. I knew that. I couldn't afford a pyrotechnic show out here within viewing distance of the castle. I also couldn't afford to use up my magic before the main event.

The emotion was so strong I felt I was covered in water up to my chin and fighting the rising tide to breathe.

"Get out of my way, Lysander," I said. My voice was as cold

and terrible as I'd ever heard it, and Lysander registered the danger in it, too. But he refused to move.

"I'd rather die than have you go in there," he said.

"Don't make me," I said. "Don't make me kill you."

The Void knew I had enough reason to. But killing someone you know; someone who is willing to die to protect you—

"Damn it, Lysander!" I shouted. "Get out of my way!"

My wand was hot in my hand, almost too hot, and my eyes filled with tears. The most irritating tears; the most infuriating. I refused to cry for a vampire. I swiped at them, trying to clear my vision.

I will not cry for a vampire.

I will not cry for a vampire.

I will not cry for a vampire.

I tried for the last time to walk around him, but he stood his ground.

"Won't let you kill yourself," he said. "Won't let you walk in on that which waits for you there."

"What waits for me?" I demanded. "You know who's waiting for me? My parents!"

Lysander's face paled further.

"Yes," I said. "I know they're alive. And I know you knew but didn't tell me."

He pushed his hair out of his face. "How could I?" he said. "You would have done exactly what you're doing now! Which is committing suicide!"

"I don't care!" I shouted back, almost doubled over by my mixed-up, rushing feelings.

"You should care," he said. "Because it's actually worse than suicide. What's waiting for you in the New Dawn Kingdom is a fate worse than death. And if you never believe anything else I ever say, so be it. But believe that."

The tears weren't going anywhere. A fresh wave stung my eyes.

"How am I supposed to do that?" I demanded. "Even if I wanted to? How am I supposed to leave them there? You don't know what it's like!" I started sobbing, and hated myself for it. "You don't know what it's like, losing your parents like that."

"I do!" yelled Lysander. "Do you think you're the only child orphaned by Acheron?"

Now there were tears in Lysander's eyes, and he clenched his teeth.

Oh, I thought. *Poor Lysander. That's the connection. That's why we're forever bonded. We feel each other's pain. Orphanos.*

I was trying my best to fend off the sobbing, but the deep ache in my throat radiated out and I found it difficult to control the crying. I had to pull myself together and get into the castle.

I took a deep breath and held my wand out toward Lysander. I had to go and he was in my way. I had to harden my heart against him if I had any hope of saving my parents.

THE GHOSTS around me started saying my thoughts out loud, a cacophony of whispered angry chants. Their voices swirled round me, white mist versus black.

He lied to you.

He set you up.

He trapped you.

He didn't tell you your parents were alive.

I pushed away the memories of him saving my life in the Olde Worlde steam train, and at the EverShade market. I pushed away the memory of that venom-fueled night that would shame me till my dying day. The night Lysander didn't take advantage when I offered him my neck.

"You lied to me," I said. I held out my mother's antique wand. It was burning my skin. It became so hot that I exclaimed and dropped it on the dark soil we were standing on.

Inherited wands sometimes had a mind of their own, but my mother's had never behaved like this before. It was as if it didn't want me to hurt Lysander.

"Nano. Teflon glove." I said, and my nano flew out of my pocket and down my arm, forming a black glove. I picked up the red-hot wand and pointed it at the vampire.

"You lied to me," I said again. "You set me up."

"To protect you. To protect you, Jax!"

Harden your heart!

The murdered women echoed it: *harden your heart, harden your heart.*

"This is your last chance," I said. The wand glowed warm white in the dusk. I could feel the warmth through the glove but it could no longer burn my skin.

"I've protected you in ways you'll never know," said Lysander. "I've always been in the shadows, watching out for you."

"Why?" I demanded, my voice gruff with emotion.

"I'll tell you everything I know," said Lysander, holding a gentle hand out to me. "Come away with me now. Away from here."

"Tell me now or get out of my way," I said.

Harden your heart.

The lump in my throat was glowing as bright as my wand.

"I'm not moving, Jax," said Lysander. "If my last living moment is spent protecting you, it will be well spent."

CHAPTER 25
CHOIR OF GHOSTS

Tried to quieten the hammering of my heart. I tried to ignore the rustling voices that emanated from the specters who shimmered around me. I failed at both.

I held out my white-hot wand for the third time, aimed it at Lysander, and allowed the magic to gather in my chest like electric storm clouds. I steadied my breathing and felt the power in my arms, my hands, my fingers. I felt as if I had sparks in my brain.

Lysander stood his ground and looked at me with a grim expression. I could see he was clenching and unclenching his jaw. I saw the fear in his eyes, but it was combined with a kind of acceptance, as if he had expected this to happen. His arms fell to his sides in surrender.

The emotions built and built until I felt like I could not hold them in any longer, and my skin was alight with magic. The ghosts whispered in so many different voices I felt like I was going insane.

"*Fiat fulgur!*" I yelled, and the wand exploded in my hand, sending a shower of hot sparks into my eyes and face.

I shouted in fright, and was temporarily blinded. I patted my hair and face, thinking I was on fire, but I wasn't. The red hot poker began to cool on the ground.

Lysander stepped forward. "Are you all right?"

I don't need a wand to do this, I thought. *Especially not a wand with a mind of its own.*

I removed the glove and threw it on the ground alongside the rebellious spell stick. I drew myself up and readied my hands to do the magic my wand had refused to do. It was difficult to look into Lysander's eyes, but I forced myself to do it. The dead women urged me on.

He killed us, they whispered.

"*Ignem exquiris!*" I yelled, and this time the fiery orange blasted out of my hands and slammed into Lysander's chest.

That's for Liz Durison, I thought.

He shouted in pain but didn't retreat.

"*Ignem exquiris!*" I shouted again, and a new torrent of fire smashed into him, and he dropped to his knees.

That's for the other women.

I tried one last time to get past him and he grabbed my ankle, tripping me up. I fell down onto the soft ground.

He lied to you.

He set you up.

He trapped you.

Harden your heart.

I kicked at him to let me go, but he held on. I needed to get into the castle. I needed to save my parents. I had no choice but to end it, right there and then.

"Fiat fulgur!" I shouted.

The pain I was feeling blasted out of me in a potent white-blue current, spearing Lysander directly in the heart. He screamed in pain and clutched his chest; his face contorting in agony. I let out a sob; I couldn't help it. I tried to crawl away but still he held on. I turned back, knees in the dead leaves and mud.

"Fiat fulgur!"

This time it was a sob. A lone murmur from my lips supported by a dozen whispers from a dozen pairs of blue spectral lips. A wave of electricity smashed Lysander to the ground, and when I saw the embers begin to flicker under his skin I knew it was over. His skin turned from pale to glowing, like a piece of white paper above a flame, and then the skin-paper caught and there were sparks and racing orange threads of fire as the heat consumed him; slowly at first and then too quickly, and his body crumpled in on itself and burst into meter-high flames, a fireball, a sun. I lifted my arms, covering my eyes to protect them from the blast, but I still felt it on my skin and deep inside my body.

I felt the heat on my face. It quickly faded; a spent star. When I opened my eyes again the choir of ghosts was gone and Lysander was crumpling into cinders and ash, and I felt as if I was crumpling, too. I doubled over onto the dark soil and got a mouth full of dirt, but I didn't care.

Something was searing inside me, as if I was on fire alongside the vampire, but he was turning into ash while my lungs were still ballooning, my heart pounding. I was alive, but it felt like my insides were dying. As if I was being scraped out from inside myself and I was all alone, as lonely as I had ever been, lying there on the cold ground beside the ash.

The sobbing began again, a loud, violent sound that I couldn't believe was coming from me, and it echoed in the bleak fading light. A hardness in my throat like a glowing coal that flared and then died away slowly, slowly, as I sobbed and sobbed into the dead leaves. The dirt and ash coated my skin. With numb fingers I clipped my wand back in place.

Why did it hurt so much?

I didn't know. All I could do was clutch at the cold ground until it faded. I closed my eyes, and the darkness overcame me.

CHAPTER 26

THE CORNER OF THE ROOM

When I opened my eyes again, it was another childhood memory dream. I was standing on our front lawn, just back from the neighbor's party next door. I could still taste the Oros juice and the Cheese Curls, the popcorn and cake. I knew which day that was. Every moment of it was engraved into my psyche, every split-second. The yellow shorts I was wearing, the *My Little Pony* shirt. I didn't want to walk any farther. I knew what awaited me. I'd had this dream a thousand times. I'd remembered the pain more than that.

I didn't want to step forward, but something forced me to, and soon I saw my strawberry glitter jelly sandals swinging out before me and I walked toward the front door.

SOMETHING WAS DIFFERENT. *Something was wrong. I knew it before I even entered the house. That was the first time I smelled that scent. The one I know so well, now. The smell that fills me with dread and dangerous thoughts.*

Crimson copper.

I called for my parents and looked in the kitchen for them, in the garden, in the study, but they didn't answer. Their bedroom door was closed. I knocked on it.

"Mom?" I said. "Dad?"

Still no answer.

I stood there for a while, not sure what to do. Perhaps they were sleeping. I tried the handle, but the door was locked.

"Mom?"

Starting to get worried, I dropped my party pack on the carpet and wrapped my fingers around the doorknob. The metallic blood smell was much stronger now, and I knew for sure something was wrong. I had never melted a lock before. Mom and Dad had told me that I was only to do it in an emergency. I wasn't sure if it was an emergency, but it felt like one.

"Ignem exquiris," I said, and the heat from my hand softened the metal of the lock just enough for me to push the door open.

No child should have to see what I did when I opened that door. My parents lay there, lifeless, on their bed, their skin as pale as paper. There were red blooms on their pillows where their wounds had stained the cotton. I didn't understand. My mind raced and stumbled. I couldn't make sense of what I was seeing. I stepped closer, took my mother's cold hand, and searched her face for some kind of answer. She had two dark holes in her neck, a thin line joining them. Dad had the same.

Inside I was panicking, but on the outside I was too shocked to cry or scream or do anything but stand there and look at their near-transparent skin.

Finally, the panic inside my body exploded to the outside, too, and I started to move. I took my mother's precious silver wand from her hand, and my dad's pentacle ring from his finger. I would need all the help I could get, I realized, my organs as heavy as lead, because from now on I was alone in the world. And it was a dangerous world.

I looked for the last time into my mom's startled Pacific blue eyes, which were staring at the ceiling, unblinking, and I closed the lids. A sob rose in my throat, but I swallowed it down. Now was the time to be strong. I closed my dad's eyes, too, and that's when I saw the vampire standing in the corner of the room.

He had been there all along, watching me, as still as glass. His face was a mask of evil, his hair black as tar. A jagged scar ran up from his left eye, past his hairline and into his scalp. An hour passed in that split-second. An hour of us standing there, regarding each other, deciding what to do next. An hour of me being within touching distance of my forever-sleeping parents who had loved me fiercely and without wavering, and their cold-blooded killer. A lifetime of love that was lost to me forever.

I forced myself to breathe, and I looked Acheron in the eyes. This time I wouldn't run.

CHAPTER 27
HE WALKED THROUGH FIRE

I'd relived that moment over and over, wondering if I should have done this, or should have done that. The guilt I felt for just bolting out of there forever stained me, and I spent a lifetime trying to make up for it, as my bedpost bears witness.

Mom and Dad looked dead, or I was sure I wouldn't have left them. The truth—that they were still alive—simultaneously hurt me and filled me with tentative hope. What had been done to them in the intervening twenty years? What had they been through? Could I have saved them? I thought I'd never get the chance to find out, but there I was, standing in their bedroom, copper crimson mist in the air, and Acheron in the corner.

He looked slightly older, but had that eternal-youth, eternal-death thing going on that vampires do. Beautiful, repulsive skin. And that scar—that scar I'd seen every day since that terror-filled moment I lost my parents.

"Acheron," I said. He may have aged, but I was still a child. My voice sounded impossibly young. Had I ever been that innocent, that tender?

"Jacquelyn," he said.

I didn't have my crossbow on my back, and my trench coat had yet to be invented. A world of pain lay ahead of me before I would finally get to meet Matron Ferra at Copperfield and get taken under her wing. But I had a feeling we weren't going to get that far. Little girls don't win battles against cold-hearted vampires.

By choosing to stay and fight, I had chosen death.

We stood and stared at each other, my parents' pale unmoving bodies our only audience. I had my mother's wand in my right hand and my father's ring in my left. I felt the pain and anger seething inside me, trying to escape, and I was ready. If I was going to die, I was going to die fighting.

"*Fiat fulgur!*" I shouted, and the blue lightning barreled out of my wand, toward Acheron.

"*Effectus adversum!*" he said, and batted the spell away with the back of his hand, as if it were nothing more than an annoying fly.

"*Fiat fulgur!*" I yelled again, and this time the lightning bolt was bigger, faster. Despite me being a child, the emotion in the room fed my magic and made it potent. The vampire swatted it away again, as if he were playing a rather boring game of table tennis. He stepped forward and my heart raced. He was going to kill me.

"Ignem exquiris!" I shouted, and a comet of yellow fire rushed at him, blasting him in the face, showering his whole body and cape with yellow and blue flames.

Acheron didn't bat an eyelid. He walked through fire as if it were air.

I screamed as he came toward me. My childish instinct was to run to my parents seeking their shelter, but the sight of their white sheets, blooming with blood, made me freeze.

"Ignem exquiris!" I rasped, my voice almost lost in terror. Another comet smashed into Acheron, but he didn't feel it. He kept coming. He was a meter away from me, half a meter.

"Fiat fulgur!" I shouted, but he smashed the spell back at me, and at such close quarters the lightning spell hit me hard, electrocuting me where I stood. My body radiated with a white hot pain; I felt the current in every limb, every digit, blasting my nerves and cauterizing blood vessels, causing my heart to fibrillate and lean on the very edge of stopping for good.

"Children shouldn't play with lightning," he said. The electric current had short-circuited my brain and the world went fuzzy at the edges.

I fainted, and he caught me just before I hit the ground. Acheron looked into my closing eyes and brought his hand up. He touched my forehead, a light tap between my brows, and everything disappeared.

CHAPTER 28

DARK STONE SHELL

When I woke up every part of my body hurt, and my mouth was so dry I could hardly swallow. I checked to see if Gizmo was okay, but he was no longer in my pocket. I got a fright, thinking that he may have taken the brunt of that lightning spell, but then I remembered I hadn't been wearing my trench coat when Acheron had turned my magic against me. Turns out that a *My Little Pony* shirt did little to fend off the attack of the most evil vampire in the Realm.

Gizmo had probably been spared. At least that was something, I thought, as I blinked at the dark stone ceiling above me. The air was frigid, and there was the sound of dripping water. I guessed that I was in one of Acheron's dungeons. I lay there on the slab of rock, listening to the dripping sound, trying to get some feeling back into my wrecked body. It was the first time I had been hit by an almost full-on *exquiris* and I hoped to the Void that it would be the last. I doubted my body could take another shock like that. What made it worse was that it had been my own magic. It was like a magical own-goal, and all wizards knew that they always hurt more.

I stretched and groaned, and felt simultaneous numbness and pain throughout my shattered body. When I tried to lever myself up, I realized that my muscles weren't taking orders. It was as if the connection between my brain and my seared nerves was severed. I tried again, and there was very little movement. I gave myself a few minutes' break, and then tried once more to sit up. This time it worked, but there was still something holding me back.

I felt something against my neck, and an acute stabbing pain, as if I had a razor blade lodged in there.

"What?" I said, but no sound came out. It was like a silent cough. The blade, or whatever it was, tore at the flesh in my neck. I became flustered then, panicky, and I felt I needed to remove the thing immediately. I clutched at it and ripped it out, and a fountain of blood spurted from the hole it left in my neck. Of course, I realized what it was just a second before I looked at it.

A jugular hook. The same device used to siphon the blood from bleedfarm victims, the same device used to drain my parents to the point of oblivion. Once I had torn out the medical fang, the blood kept shooting out of my neck and I knew I had to stop it.

"Nano. Tourniquet." My voice was raw and almost inaudible, but the nano understood and whipped around my neck, and knotted itself tightly there, controlling the bleeding. I could still feel the throbbing, but when I felt the fabric that was covering the wound, my fingers came away dry.

I looked at the red-stained hook in my hand, and felt the familiar feeling of disgust I had for vampires. How they ruthlessly attacked and killed and orphaned people, and despite my sorry state I felt my magic building up again.

I sat up and took in the sparse interior décor of the dungeon. I blinked and waited for my eyes to adjust to the dim light. There was nothing to see except four dark gray walls of stone, damp and ancient-looking. The IV tube that had been carrying my blood to a silicone bag on the floor lay like a thin dead snake. I threw the fang down to join it, and tried to rub the blood off my hands.

ONCE I FELT ready to stand, I pulled my legs over and levered myself slowly off the slab and into a standing position. It hurt, but it was also a relief to be off the cold stone, which had leeched my body of feeling and warmth. I stood still for a moment, holding onto the stone, making sure I wasn't too dizzy to walk. When I felt reasonably confident I stepped away from it. My legs were wobbly, my knees were jelly, and I had dull fireworks cracking in my head, but apart from that I felt like a million bucks. I was alive, which was an unexpected bonus, and I was closer to the New Dawn Throne than I had ever been. I was in a unique position to take down the vile leader of the Silvano Clan, Acheron Baldassare, the vampire who had ripped my life away from me. More importantly, I was about to meet my parents again for the first time in twenty years. I realized I probably wouldn't come out of it alive, but the Grim Reaper had been my number one stalker for a while now, and I was pretty sure he was getting impatient. He wanted the goods, and my body was close to giving up the ghost. I was living on borrowed time; had been for weeks, ever since Darick had been sent to assassinate me. I understood my fate. It was so clear, as if it were a bright billboard right there in the dungeon. I'd save my parents, I'd destroy the New Dawn Kingdom, and I'd die in the process. If that's what it cost me, I was willing to pay.

There was no mental bandwidth for sadness then, or regret. I couldn't think of the life I may have had with Darick, and our —imaginary—sweet little apple-cheeked baby. There was no time to think of my best friend or my dwarf fairy godmother or my favorite goblin, or Bron or Gizmo or the Belore twins.

The only thing I had energy to focus on were those two things.

My parents.

The throne.

I had a job to do. This would sustain me.

I looked around at the dungeon again. No windows. Just a black metal door which undoubtedly had a security enchantment on it. I stepped up to it and ran my palms over the cool steel.

"Orc steel," I said. "Practically unbreakable."

I spoke out loud. Maybe because I was used to having Gizmo to chat to, or maybe because after everything I'd been through, I was now probably one crayon short of a coloring box. Maybe it was just comforting to hear something rather than nothing in that dark stone shell.

Of course, you didn't need to break something to get around it. The paranormal life has taught me that much. The door wasn't really the problem, I thought, unclipping my wand with an unsteady hand. It was whatever was behind the door.

CHAPTER 29
FEVER TORCH

I couldn't afford to make too much noise, or whoever was guarding this dungeon would grab me. Subtle magic was usually not my forté, but I had little choice.

"Ignem exquiris," I said softly, looking at the tip of my wand. A small flame flicked into existence. I needed it to get hotter. A lot hotter. I squeezed my eyes shut and tried to remember my Copperfield Latin lessons with old Bent Neck. You know how they say Latin is a dead language? Professor Bendek was a living example of how dead things can be dragged into the twenty-first century. We would have called him a coffin-dodger at school but it appeared that he had hardly dodged said coffin; he had one foot squarely in there, and the other hovering indecisively above it, like a cat at an open door.

Fever. Fervor? And then I remembered.

"Fervens," I said, and the flame blazed. *"Fervens. Fervens,"* I whispered, and the flame turned from a gentle fire into the hissing blue blade of a blowtorch. Half-shielding my eyes

from the sparks, I used the fever torch to cut through the bolt that was keeping it locked. The acrid smell of molten metal filled the room. The trick worked, and as the bolt lost its bite, the door swung open toward me.

I immediately cut my magic off from the fire, and it spluttered and died.

Thank you, Professor Bent Neck, I thought, and I tentatively stepped out from my cell. There was no guard that I could see, and I immediately understood why. The dungeon was laid out like a labyrinth, a cold black maze. If someone managed to escape their cell, as I just had, they'd have to find their way through the complex maze before getting free. It would be virtually impossible to navigate, especially in the dark. There was also a disconcerting scuttling sound that made my ears itchy. I checked my pockets for Morgan's flashlight, but I no longer had it. I must have lost it somewhere between the silver-eyed zombies and the fire-breathing Komodo dragons. I'd have to use my magic to light my way, which I was hesitant to do, because I wanted to save it for the battle. I also didn't know how much Magus they had drained from me.

"*Lumos,*" I said. My still-warm wand flickered on with a glowing light.

I thought the light would make me feel better but I almost yelled with fright when I saw the walls, which were alive with scrambling black insects. A shiver ran down my spine, and my wand wobbled.

It's okay, I told myself. *It's okay. Just don't touch the walls.*

I gulped down my revulsion and fear and started walking, taking the path to my right and keeping my arms glued close to my ribs. There was a heavy scraping sound, and when I stopped to look back, the maze had shifted its walls, rearranging itself behind me. Insects scuttled and shrieked.

I never needed Gizmo like I needed him at that moment. It felt absolutely impossible to make it through the maze.

WWGD.

What Would Gizmo Do?

I kept walking, turning left and right when my instinct told me to, the stone walls shifting around me all the time. I tried to ignore the beetles crunching under my boots like nut shells, and the ones climbing up my legs, but my anxiety climbed with every corner. After walking for around twenty minutes, I understood that there was no way out. Of course there was no way out. I was Acheron's prisoner, and he was not going to make escaping easy.

I slowed to a stop, not knowing what to do, but that gave the insects more of an opportunity to climb onto me, so I carried on. Maybe the point of this maze was to exhaust the captive. If it was, it was working. I felt like I was going insane, that this was what it would feel like to be mad, to be stuck in an eternal shifting maze with no way out. Still, I kept walking.

HOURS LATER—OR maybe days, or minutes—I'd lost all sense of time—I found myself walking in a stupor, as if I were sleepwalking. My eyes were half closed, my legs kept walking, and my mind was on autopilot. It was the only way I could keep going. I could feel the stinging of burst blisters on my feet, and my head was pounding as I took turn after turn, stumbling along into a special brand of insanity.

Then I heard something. It immediately snapped me out of my lethargic shuffling. A woman's voice. Or, more precisely, a woman's groan. She was in pain. I increased my pace, listening for the sound, which had finally given me some kind of direction. My heart began banging in my chest. I knew who it was. Dared I hope? I had no choice; the hope was already there, blazing from inside my ribcage.

"Mom?" I said, quietly at first. The groaning stopped. "Mom?"

There was muffled speech. More than one person.

"What?" I heard someone say.

"Who's there?" said the other.

"Mom?" I shouted. "Dad?"

I heard a sob, and the sound hit me hard in the throat, and I sobbed, too.

It might not be them, I told myself. *Easy. Easy. It might be a trap. A trick.*

I ran toward the voices.

CHAPTER 30
THE SHAPE OF A PARENT

When I arrived at the doorway of where the voices were coming from—a monstrous maw of a doorway, with rotten teeth like an orc's jaw—I forgot about my intent to keep my magic slow and subtle.

"Fiat fulgur!" I shouted, and a vicious blue lightning bolt crashed out of my wand and smashed into the lock.

"Stand back!" I shouted—a little late, I suppose—and I lifted my knee and kicked the door with all my might. The whole sheet of metal came off its hinges and slammed to the floor. I searched the dark cell for the bodies I knew were there.

I saw the two of them, backs against the wall and cowering, shielding their faces from me. Even in the dark, and with their faces covered, they were immediately recognizable. A child never forgets the shape of a parent. The details may be fuzzy, but I knew without a doubt that they were my mother and father.

The child inside me wanted to drop to her knees and sob, overwhelmed by the emotion of seeing her twenty-year-dead parents alive and so obviously suffering. But I was no longer a child. I was no longer an orphan.

"Dad!" I shouted, and I grabbed him. "Mom!" They both flinched. I didn't blame them. It was even more frightening for them than it was for me.

Slowly, ever so slowly, they lowered their hands, until I could see their eyes, and they could see mine. I cried out in shock and sorrow.

"What has he done to you?" I whispered.

They both had that chalky skin that Slyden Abarim had, and the black veins around their eyes. What frightened me most was the emptiness in their eyes, as if Death had already been and taken what he wanted, and left the rest behind. They looked aged and ill beyond their years, and I fell down on my knees, and wept.

My first cries came out at almost a scream, so intense was my fear and grief. It sounded like there was a wild animal inside me, howling and shrieking to get out. It was a nightmare beyond my worst nightmare. Losing my parents to death twenty years ago was terrible. Losing them to decades of suffering was far worse. Twenty years of torture. I couldn't bear it.

They didn't leave me to my grieving. They pulled me up with cold, stiff hands and squeezed my cheeks, staring and prodding and lifting me off the stone floor.

"Jacquelyn!" they rasped. "Jacquelyn!"

I saw the stents in their necks, where the vampires had been siphoning their blood all this time, building up enough Magus to build the New Dawn Kingdom. My hand flew up to the hole in my own neck, which was still covered tightly by the tourniquet.

Blood Magic.

Keeping them barely alive, just breathing, just enough to keep stealing their blood. They were painfully thin, and as pale as the moon. Their empty eyes kept shocking me, as if they carried small electric currents in their gaze.

"I would have looked for you," I sobbed. "I would have spent every minute looking for you, if I had known you were alive."

Perhaps a small part of me had known they were alive, and I had always dismissed it as childish denial. Perhaps that was the reason I had become a detective, driven to find people and things.

They just kept uttering my name and touching my face, and as my crying subsided I felt their hands grow warmer, and their faces flushed with the slightest tint of color. It could have been hope, or imagination, but I thought I saw a flicker of emotion in their formerly stagnant eyes.

They were dying. That was plain to see. But they were also coming back to life.

"You must leave," said my mother. "You must leave before he does to you what he did to us."

"I will leave," I said. "And I'll take you with me. I'll take you home."

I didn't know where "home" was, but I'd be happy to take them anywhere but that cold scuttling dungeon under the shadow of Acheron. Suddenly I didn't feel up to battling the vampires. All I wanted was to steal away from there and set my parents up somewhere warm and safe. But I knew that would be impossible for as long as Acheron existed. There was only one way to save my parents, and that was to save the Realm.

"I HAVE SO MANY QUESTIONS," I said.

"Of course you do," said my father.

"We have questions, too," said Mom. "Not a day passes that your father and I don't talk about you. We'd daydream about what you looked like, and what you were doing. And look at you now," she said, and then sobs started crashing out of her mouth, and Dad pulled her close and clenched his jaw. She forced her words past the tears. "Look at you, Jax. You're everything, and more."

We huddled there, hugging, until Mom stopped shaking and heaving.

Where do I start? I thought. I wanted to know absolutely everything, but I didn't know how much time we had.

"That day," I said, holding back the tears. "That day you were attacked. It was Acheron."

"Yes," said my father. "He's had this kingdom planned for ... longer than you've been alive."

"I know," I said. "I found an old book. *Vampiric Lore,* by Zolastaro. It set out—"

My father's grim face blinked at me, and then his chapped lips turned up into a smile. I didn't finish my sentence.

"It worked," he said, and I just looked at him. His eyes shone with tears.

"What worked?"

My mother also smiled now, and they looked at each other and grinned.

"It worked," said my mother, and I could swear she almost chuckled.

Gradually, the line of dominoes in my mind fell.

My haunted apartment. Ghost. When he wasn't artfully rearranging my reading matter he was doing my laundry. What was one of the most cherished memories I had of my father? That absolutely ordinary day that I always remembered whenever I smelled laundry detergent. I zipped back in time to when I was a little girl, standing in our family kitchen.

SUNSHINE STREAMING THROUGH THE WINDOWS, the kettle singing for tea. Mom slicing bread. Dad coming in from collecting the washing off the line outside, and playfully lobbing a clean sock at me. It landed on my head, and as I tried to grab it, I missed, and it dropped down to the floor. I looked up at him, and we both giggled.

MY APARTMENT MAY BE DESTROYED, but I hadn't lost Ghost. I had found Ghost. He was standing right in front of me.

"That was you?" I asked. "All that time?"

He was still smiling. "It was the only way I could look after you."

"How?" I asked. "How did you do it?" Wizards couldn't teleport their spirits like that, especially sick wizards without their magical instruments. "Wizards can't do that."

Their smiles faded. "Pureblood wizards can't do that," my mother said. "Your father is—"

"Different," he said, firmly.

"Different?" My only memories of them were as wizards.

Different, how? Half djinn? Half werewolf? Half—

"No," I said, as the reality sunk in. I shifted backwards, away from him.

"There's nothing to be afraid of, Jax," said my mother. "Not in here."

I swallowed hard, and tried to calm my heart, which had decided it very much wanted to beat itself all the way out my chest.

"No," I said again. I couldn't believe it. I didn't want to believe it. But it made sense. I covered my face with my hands as the cold dread clung to me.

My father spoke gently. "Do you know," he said slowly, "do you know what a Dhampyr is?"

CHAPTER 31
WAX PAPER ON SKELETONS

I flinched, as if the word had barbed my skin, barbed my heart.

Of course I knew what a dhampyr was.

"Don't say it," I begged him, speaking through my fingers. "Don't say it." I had the feeling that if he said it out loud my whole world would crumble.

SOMETIMES YOUR DESTINY unfolds before you and you just want to set it on fire.

EVERY VAMPIRE SLAYER worth their wooden stake and garlic wreath knows what a dhampyr is, because dhampyrs are the original vampire slayers.

"A dhampyr is half human, and half vampire," he said. "It's

no wonder you chose the profession you did. No wonder you're so strong, and resilient."

No wonder I can cope with very little sleep and food.

No wonder I can step out of windows and fly from building to building.

No wonder I am immune to mesmerization.

I was crying again, I couldn't help it. I felt as if I'd been kicked in the stomach.

How could my father, the most revered human in my life, be a vampire? How could I?

"No," I mumbled, my face and hands wet with hot tears. "No, no, no."

Impossible. Impossible *that I was forever tied to the creatures I hated more than anything.*

"It's difficult to hear, I know," said my mother. "But it's a good thing, really."

I took my hands away and looked at her, demanding an explanation.

"The blend of our blood—your Dad's and mine—is extremely powerful," she said. "It's why Acheron was in our bedroom that day. The reason we were selected to be brought here."

I WAS STILL STRUGGLING with my own new status as a mixed-blood to take in other details. I was beyond shocked and appalled that I had dirty vampire blood running through my veins. I imagined my heart pumping black blood, oily and slick, pushing it through my body, contaminating me with its evil. I wished I could tear it out. I had never felt such self-hatred before.

But Mom was right. There was a silver lining. It's well known in the touched world that hybrids have "superpowers." Blended Bloods are a cut above regular purebloods because they inherit power from both species. A cross between a werewolf and a witch, for example, would have the strength of a wolf, and the cunning of a witch. If Isadora Crowe and Laurent were to have children, they'd definitely be on the A-team.

My breath was shaking, my throat ached. It was a lot to take in. I had to push the barreling steam train of thoughts aside and focus again on my mission impossible.

Get my parents home.

Destroy the New Dawn Kingdom.

"I need to get you out of here," I said to them. "But I don't know how."

They glanced at each other with a sad smile.

"Oh, Jacquelyn," said my mother. "We didn't show you the way here for you to save us. We did it so that you could save yourself."

Dad cleared his throat. "I'm sorry we're telling you so many difficult things today, but the truth is—"

"We're dying," said Mom. "We've been dying for a long time."

"No," I said. "You're not. You're alive. You're living."

"Look at us," said my mother, sternly. "Jax. Look at us."

They were wax paper on skeletons. It was plain to see that there was nothing left of them. But I refused to give up. I had just found them; no way was I going to let them die.

"You're breathing," I said. "All you need to do is keep breathing. I'm going to get you out of here."

"Getting out of the kingdom will be difficult—"

"Almost impossible."

"—even for a strong, healthy person."

I thought of the obstacle course Acheron had set up for me. Crawling through the tunnel from The Copper Cog, the volcanic island with angry reptiles and sinking sand. The haunted forest, the terrifying cemetery of Obsidian Hill. And that was just the scenery. That was before anyone got hold of us: vampires, orcs, gray-skinned goblins.

"We've been hanging on for years," said my father. "Hanging on in the hope of seeing you again."

Mom looked at me with her dull, pained eyes. "We spoke about giving up, about never seeing you again, and we couldn't let that happen."

"We even wondered if we *should* die to cut off the Magus

supply to the kingdom. But then we realized that if we did that, you'd be the one they'd replace us with."

I wasn't going to tell them what they wanted to hear. That I would leave them to die in peace. It wasn't going to happen. My mind whirred with ideas about what to do next.

How would we get out of this dungeon?

"You've tried to escape?" I asked.

"Everything," said my father. "Everything you could think of. And we've had a lot of time to think."

My parents shared that wry smile again, and I realized where I got my knack of joking in even the worst situations. I also saw that I had my father's eyes, and my mother's hair. My father's jaw, my mother's shoulders. I could stare at them all day, seeking out the nuances of appearance they had passed down to me, along with their potent magic.

"I want to know everything about you," I said.

"We want you to tell us everything about yourself, too," Dad said. "I was only able to get a vague sense of you when I visited your apartment. By the time we were finally able to get the spell right, our magic was very weak."

"It took a whole day for us to gather the momentum to push that bloody book off the shelf," said Mom. There was humor in her eyes. I hugged them both, and cringed inwardly when I felt their knobby bones and wasted-away flesh.

There would be no time for the kind of discovery I wanted. I craved to know every detail about them and about our family home. I wanted to tell them about the Ferals and my days at Copperfield, and about Ferra's steady wing, and her steampunk pub for magical creatures. There was so much to talk about.

We all jumped when we noticed the shadow in the doorway. The silhouette of a towering orc was inspecting the ripped hinges. When he stepped into the dim light of the cell, I recognized the skinhead. It was the Hammerskin commander general, in full uniform. He looked directly at me with his evil yellow eyes. When he opened his mouth the ferocity of his death-breath almost bowled me over.

"Jacquelyn Denna Knight," he drawled through moist lips. "I've been looking for you."

CHAPTER 32
MOVING MAZE

"You'd think an old fortress like Alcazar wouldn't have security cameras," the Hammerskin commander general said. He didn't have to conclude his sentence. The repercussions were clear. The teetotaling general had played back the videos of what had happened the night of the Magra-Khargol wedding. He'd seen Shagar and I drag Raguk's body along the flagstone passage and dump him into the basement below the hidden trapdoor. He'd seen my glamour potion wear off and my body transform from orc wet nurse back to wily wizard. And he wouldn't even have needed the security cameras to see the purple tinge on the bottom of the champagne corks, the sign of Indigo Violent being injected into each individual bottle—apart from the wedding couple's, which had been specially marked with a heart on the label—and work out that it was that poison that had killed most of his army in the great banquet hall.

"I thought you might find me," I said. "But unfortunately for you, Acheron Baldassare wants me alive."

The general grunted. His face was pulled into an ugly sneer. He couldn't touch me, and he knew it.

"Come," he said, curling his hairy bratwurst fingers at me.

"I'm not going with you," I said, shaking my head. "No way."

"You don't have a choice, wizard," he said. "Come. All of you. Baldassare's orders."

I spotted more movement at the door. More orcs. No wonder there were no more Hammerskins left in the Realm. Most were dead, and the ones who weren't were guarding the New Dawn castle. The general's presence came as no surprise. He knew which side of his bread was buttered.

"We can do this the hard way, if you like," he said, and whistled for his men, who stepped into the cell with barbed baseball bats and crudely fashioned knives.

I wasn't going to give him a reason to rough me up. I lifted my hands in surrender. "We'll come with you."

"Take them to Baldassare," he told his second in command.

The orc nodded, but looked nervous. "You're not coming with us?"

"I'm going ahead to brief the squad at the castle. We weren't expecting the wizard to arrive so soon."

"Yes, sir."

"What?" grunted the general. "You're scared? Of a girl wizard?"

"No, sir," he said. But the Hammerskin eyed me warily. Of course, there would be stories about me, shaking up the orc grapevine. Some maybe truer than others. A wizard who slew the Hammerskin army single-handedly with some kind of poisonous magic. A wizard who also happened to be hanging around when the Orc Godfather had been killed. A wizard who barbecued orc nipples and fed them to her pet ferret for breakfast.

Orcs were suspicious and paranoid at the best of times, and I could see that this one didn't like the idea of spending quality time with me.

THE COMMANDER GENERAL left the cell, and I saw the maze magically move around him as he walked, as if he were an opposing magnet and the black rocks were made of steel. It was a nifty spell, and I was actually glad to be escorted out of there, because I'd had no clue at all how to escape on my own. My parents hesitated in leaving. They looked around at the blank walls of the cell. It looked like nothing to me, but it had been their life for the last twenty years, and we all knew they'd never see it again.

No fewer than six guards walked with us, one in front, one at the back, and two on either side to keep us from running. My parents' walking was painfully slow, and I ordered an orc to help them. Surprisingly, he agreed. I looked at the back of their greasy skinheads as we walked. They all bore the same tattoo, the one I had come to know so well. The symbol of hatred and division, and cold-blooded violence.

It took ten minutes to navigate the moving maze, and then a huge door scraped open, and the cool night air cascaded over us. It was such a relief to me, who had been imprisoned for hours, and it was overwhelming for my parents, who I guessed hadn't breathed fresh air for decades. I could hear them breathing it in, could hear the rushing sound of it. What a shame, I thought, that it wasn't daytime. That they couldn't feel sunshine on their cheeks, and look at the crisp blue sky. I understood that it was never daytime here over the castle grounds. Vampires liked the weather just as it was. I looked up at the starless gray sky.

Our surrounds were shadows and black trees. There was just enough light to see the orcs around me, and the giant castle that loomed before us. It was bigger than I had imagined, and even more sinister. People had died behind those walls; I could feel their shivering spirits all around me. It was medieval-looking, and I could imagine it held torture rooms and an execution deck in the square. I had thought that the dungeon we were being held in had been dug below the castle grounds, but it turned out that Acheron didn't want his prisoners under his feet.

THE GUARDS WERE GOING to deliver us into the lion's den. I was hoping for an arrival more on my own terms, but I wasn't about to fight half a dozen orcs with nail-bats and prison shivs. Just as I had resigned myself to being presented to the most evil vampire in the land like a just-roasted chicken on a silver platter, I saw something that made me look twice.

The orc walking in front of me looked familiar. Granted, I was just looking at the back of his head, which you could argue looked exactly the same as the others. Skinheads were like that. But the way the orc moved, the slight stoop of his posture ... something about him rang a bell. Then I noticed something even odder. His Hammerskin tattoo seemed to be ... flaking off? It wasn't real ink.

What? I thought. *What?*

But before I could guess what was going on, the imposter drew a small pistol from his hip. It looked like a toy in his huge hand, but the glint of gunmetal was real. It had a silencer screwed on the end of its barrel so the gunshots sounded like lasers firing instead of gunpowder exploding. What was louder than the gunshots was the surprised yells of the Hammerskins, who didn't realize what was happening until it was too late. One by one, in quick succession and before they could run or retaliate, they each took a bullet to the head and fell backwards. The imposter was an excellent shot. This was no Neo-Nazi hauled off the street and given a stolen weapon. This was—

"Gnor?" I said. I was in wonder, and in shock. Five bodies lay on the ground around us, and his bullets had just missed my parents, who stood impossibly pale-faced and trembling. "Is that you?"

I'd recognize the Khargol loyalist anywhere. He'd been camped outside my apartment for weeks after Don Vito had promised me protection. He hadn't been the best security guard, but he seemed to be a talented marksman.

He tucked his pistol away and rubbed at his scalp, further degrading the fake tattoo. "Ergh."

"What are you doing here?" I whispered. Apart from killing Neo-Nazis, I meant.

"You released me from duty when your life was in danger," he said. I couldn't believe he could speak so well. He was using prepositions and everything. He had certainly been hiding his light under the proverbial orc bushel. The fact that he was A) awake, and B) speaking English was nothing short of a paranormal miracle.

"I released you to protect your family," I said. I had expected him to run away with them, leave the country and never come back.

Gnor dragged one of the bodies into the bushes. "I am protecting them," he said.

CHAPTER 33
DIM GRAY LIGHT

After dragging the rest of the corpses into the surrounding black-leafed fauna, Gnor explained how he had been able to shave his head and infiltrate the Hammerskins. They were always greedy for new men and had recruited him without a backward glance—or a background check. They'd sent him to the kingdom along with the rest of the remaining soldiers, and all he had to do was wait for me to arrive and volunteer to be on my detail.

"It was surprisingly easy," he said. "After the Indigo Wedding, the word spread. They're afraid of you."

"It was all Shagar," I said. "I can't take the credit."

"That may be so, but they're still scared of you," he said, and smiled. I thought his mossy tombstone teeth looked particularly pretty in the dim gray light.

Gnor knew a way into the castle around the side; a servants' entrance that was submerged in stagnant moat water.

"It stinks," he said, which was rather alarming, to be honest, coming from an orc. Even my mother's mouth fell open a little bit.

I took a minute to enjoy the moment.

The future was looking pretty *deodamn* bleak, and I probably wouldn't live to see it. I had more than ninety-nine problems, but at that moment, I was standing alongside my parents. My parents! Who were alive and who loved me, and no matter how difficult the next few hours would be, I'd always have the memory of this moment.

"You all right?" asked my father, who lay a fortifying hand on my arm. He was looking healthier, and so was Mom.

I nodded. We made our way to the much maligned moat.

WE SMELT the river before we reached it. Gnor was right. It reeked to high heaven—or whatever the equivalent of high heaven was in an upside-down pocket realm dipped in evil— and I found myself gulping down the vomit that seemed so intent on climbing up my throat.

"Holy hex," I said. "What's in there?"

Gnor shrugged. "Nothing living."

No skinny-snouted crocodiles, no razor-toothed piranhas. Not even mosquito larvae, so toxic was the sludge.

"You want us to walk in that?" I said, wrinkling my nose at the prospect of getting my boots full of the bubbling slime.

Look, I really wanted Acheron off the throne, but I had to draw a line somewhere. A wizard has to know her limitations.

"Not walk in it," Gnor said, and I was relieved. "Swim in it," he said.

"HAVE YOU DONE THIS BEFORE?" I asked Gnor.

He shook his head.

Ah, well, I thought. *Best get it over with*. I was about to take my first step into the quagmire when I felt my mother's hand hold me back.

"Stop," she said. She picked up a stone from the bank and held it up. It was smooth, and reminded me of the adder stones I had seen in the StarDust Coven case. She lobbed it into the moat, perhaps to try to ascertain how deep it was, but the stone didn't make it to the bottom. As soon as it hit the slime it dissolved with a hiss and a popping sound.

Gnor took a step backward. Perhaps he hadn't thought this through.

"Okay," I said. "I guess we'll have to go through the front door."

So, we might get shot to smithereens by the guards there, but at least we didn't have to add our skeletons to the simmering sludge soup. Another thing to be grateful for. Look at me, I thought, counting my blessings all over the place.

I looked at my parents. "You okay?"

They nodded. I was relieved to see that they were looking stronger. I unclasped the chain around my neck and removed my father's pentacle ring and gave it back to him. He began to refuse, but I put it in his palm and closed his fingers over it. I unclipped my mother's wand and gave it back to her. We were going to need all the magic we could get.

I turned to Gnor. "You need to pretend you're a Hammerskin again, and take us in as your prisoners." Hopefully that way we'd avoid being shot at first sight. "The general will be wondering where we are."

Gnor nodded. So, we'd lose the element of surprise, but we'd avoid being pumped full of lead. We were winning. Gnor slapped a Hammerskin sneer onto his usually placid face and grabbed my arm.

"Easy, tiger," I warned him. The last time he had touched me he'd dislocated my shoulder by accident.

He looked ashamed and loosened his grip.

Sorry, his eyes said. *I was just getting into character.*

I remembered the flaking tattoo on his scalp. It was a dead giveaway—"dead" being the operative word.

"Wait," I said. I felt my neck. I was sure it had stopped bleeding. "Nano," I said. "Gnor, cap."

My nano untied itself from my neck. I felt the blood rush back to my skin but the wound did not bleed. The nano pulled itself into a cap and landed neatly on the Khargol's head.

We trekked along through the swirling black mist, stumbling over fallen branches and spiteful rocks. As we approached the behemoth building I couldn't help but be awed by it. The palace was larger than any building I'd ever seen, and its spires reached right into the clouds. The gray exterior had a gradient to it, as if it had been standing for centuries against wind and storms. Every flagpole had a teal silk ribbon flying from it, and large swathes of the fabric hung from the sides, too. The banners were the same teal color as the inside of the Silvano capes, and the same symbol we'd seen branded on the V-Cult victims. "Vampire Anarchy" was my thought on seeing that icon for the first time back in the city morgue, and I hadn't been far wrong.

I felt a twinge for Lysander, but I did my best to ignore it. The dead women had demanded justice, and I had delivered it. Still, I felt a needle in my heart.

WHEN THE GUARDS at the front of the castle spotted us they yelled and waved their AK47s, trumpeting to the others that we had arrived. They looked more like a ragtag band of Somali pirates than royal palace guards.

The commander general stepped forward with folded arms, his military uniform glinting with pins and badges.

"What took you so long?" he growled. "And where are the others?"

"We heard a noise," said Gnor, gesturing behind us with a flick of his head. "The others went to patrol."

"Fine," said the general, but I saw the suspicion sparkle in his eyes. "Bring them in. Baldassare is waiting."

WALKING through the castle reminded me of being in Alcazar, and I shuddered. I'd had enough of medieval fairs and fortresses and citadels. The interior of the palace was even spookier than the exterior. Countless vampires silently swarmed the walls. They watched, wordless, as we passed. Greek and Roman sculptures lined the halls, and they watched us, too. The castle was draughty, but I could still smell the vampires and the orcs and I felt sickened by it.

My nerves were scratching into me, making my hands perspire and my stomach cramp. I wished we could walk a little longer, so that I could get a handle on my anxiety, but the general stopped outside a giant carved timber door. It had beasts carved into it, and tortured people. It reminded me of the Morninglark Harp, and that 15th century painting of hell by Hieronymus Bosch, and the silver-eyed zombies. Two armed orcs stood on either side, and the general nodded at them. They removed the plank from the doors with a clank and pushed them open.

CHAPTER 34
BOLD BLOOD ARROW

Acheron Baldassare, most ruthless of vampires, leader of the Silvano Clan, king of the New Dawn Kingdom, slouched regally on his custom-built throne. It was fashioned from wizard staffs and witches' wands; elf femurs, dwarf gold, and stolen fae jewels. A huge pair of black wings stretched out from the back of the chair as if about to take flight, and its charcoal-colored griffin feathers vibrated almost imperceptibly in the draught. It was a terrible thing to behold, grand and cruel.

The HighFire Crown was sparkling on Acheron's head, and his facial scar was still visible, but faded, thanks to the Crown's healing magic. He was larger than life in every way, as if he had grown inflated along with his ego. Teal banners hung from the walls and a glorious red carpet—like a bold blood arrow—showed us the way to walk and to kneel. I could smell him, his particular scent of copper crimson mist.

"Ah," he said, his voice sounding like the purr of a post-kill jaguar. "Finally. You've arrived."

He interlaced his fingers and rested them on his lap, smiling at us, showing us his fangs. Ice chinked down my spine. Evil radiated off the vampire in waves, evil I'd never felt so strongly before, like a repulsive yellow stink. The doors were locked behind us.

He probably wanted to be addressed as "Your Royal Highness" or "King Acheron" or, at the very least, "Sir," but I wasn't going to give him the satisfaction. He certainly wouldn't appreciate the nickname for him I'd picked up from Zolastaro. I wondered briefly what his reaction would be if I yelled over at him: *Yo, Bald Ass! Whatcha gonna do?*

Acheron snapped his fingers, and one of his men appeared by his side. Not a Neo-Nazi minion, but a rather distinguished-looking vampire. I recognized him immediately. I'd know that greased-back Dracula hairstyle anywhere.

"Demetrius," said Acheron. "Please reveal to Ms. Knight what we have for her."

He was definitely putting on a show. I've never in my life known a vampire to say "please" or "thank you."

Demetrius stared at me for a moment, and then, with a flick of his wrist, he removed an invisibility curtain and revealed a woman strapped to a chair.

Morgan!

It was as if Acheron had somehow been able to access that nightmare I'd had where Morgan had been gagged and strapped to a chair just before Demetrius had bitten her. I saw the same hungry look on his face as he gently touched a strand of her hair, and my adrenaline climbed as I realized what he was planning.

I wondered when and where they had captured her, and where Darick was. I could really do with an expert assassin on my side, I thought. It would make it extra satisfying if the man Acheron had hired to kill me was the one to get us out of here.

Morgan's eyes were wide and glassy, but she wasn't struggling. My guess was that she'd been trying to escape for hours and was now virtually comatose from fear and exhaustion. I hated seeing her like that, so terrified, and my anger began to crowd out my fright. All the people this man had killed, all the lives stolen. My fury grew and grew like a stoked fire. The presence of my ill parents behind me shored me up and made me feel stronger.

You utter bastard, I wanted to say. *I grew up bereft because of you. I grew up aching and cold.*

The fury and the pain swirled within me, and I began to feel potent power rippling in my arms and fingers. I was a dhampyr, I reminded myself. A Blended Blood. I would not be ashamed. I would use it to my advantage. I had magic beyond measure. I could defeat this evil.

Of course, it was all bluster. I was as scared as anything, and I knew that Acheron was sitting on mountains of stolen magic. He had enough magic to sustain this entire upside-down realm and all the awful creatures in it; alive and dead. I was nothing on his danger radar; I was a nothing but a buzzing gnat flying into his electric forcefield. But, *deodamnatus,* I was going to try anyway.

"You have me, now," I said to Acheron. "Let Morgan go. Let my parents go. You have what you wanted. You don't need them anymore."

"You know nothing about what I need," he said.

"You need the rest of the elemental fragments. You want the Jar. You want my blood."

"I want more than that."

"I have nothing more to offer."

"You're wrong."

Oh, I thought, remembering his massive ego. "You want me to kneel."

"On the contrary," he said, and I frowned. "You still don't know who you are, do you?"

"My identity was stolen from me the day my parents were," I said. "You should know that. You were the thief."

Acheron stared at me. "Your brother didn't explain your lineage?"

"I don't have a brother," I said.

I felt, more than heard, my parents shuffle uncomfortably behind me.

"I don't have a brother," I said again, more for my own bene-fit. I would know if I had a brother. I stood there, searching through every childhood memory I had. There was no sibling. I was absolutely certain.

"Interesting," said Acheron, his lips turning up at the edges. An icy smile.

"Mom?" I said, turning just slightly toward her. I didn't want to take my eyes off Baldassare. I know just how quick and treacherous vampires can be.

I searched my mother's face, which looked pained. Dad's looked worse.

"Dad?" I said.

"We decided it was for the best," my mother said, but I could see she'd never forgiven herself for it. Her skin looked like wax paper again, and the deep hole in her neck for the stent made me cringe.

"You decided what was for the best?" I asked, not looking forward to the answer.

"I was married, before," said my father. "To a pureblood."

"To a vampire?"

"Yes. A Silvano."

The puzzle pieces slowly started spinning into place.

"When I met your mother I realized there was a better way to live. A less violent way. I left the clan and I left the woman. She never recovered from the failed marriage. She ended her own life."

My father, overcome with emotion, clamped his lips shut.

Mom continued. "Later we came to understand she had been expecting a baby during the break-up. She'd had the baby without our knowledge, and when she died, the clan took him in. He was a dear little thing. When we learnt of his existence, we wanted custody, but he was already settled there. And you had been born by then, so we decided it was best to leave him with his kin."

A little boy who had always been watching over me.

A vampire who had watched over me my whole life, until today.

The realization was a dagger twisting in my guts, flattening me, stealing my breath.

"Lysander," I whispered, and they nodded.

I forced myself to stay standing upright, even though I felt like melting to the ground.

"When Lysander was older he found out we were being held here. He'd sneak food in for us," said my mother. "And medicine. Really, he's the reason we're alive."

My heart tore like a piece of paper. "He's the reason I'm alive, too," I said.

Memories came crashing into my mind.

The blond boy that day on the street when I was sure I was going to die of the cold. He put what I thought was a blanket around me, but then I realized it was his cape.

The same boy, a year or so later, who passed me a takeaway container of food when I was so hungry I thought I would faint in the parking lot outside the discount liquor store.

The teen who I saw watching me at the Copperfield archery championship with burning coals for eyes; who cheered when I won.

The adult who saved me from Slyden Abarim on the steam train from hell; saved me from the exploding ferry; tried to save me from Acheron.

How many times had my half-brother saved my life? I'd never know.

I've always been in the shadows, he said. My eyes burned with fresh, hot tears.

CHAPTER 35
CRIMSON GOLD

"I don't know where he's gotten to," said Acheron, with a knowing glance in my direction. "It's a shame he's not here. You four could have had a little ... family reunion."

The commander general smirked. Demetrius stroked Morgan's hair, and a tear rolled down her cheek. The roving wallpaper of silent vampires trembled in my peripheral vision.

"We could have discussed your rather unique lineage," said Acheron. "And the reason you're here today."

I talked past the molten lump in my throat. "I know why I'm here."

Acheron stood up and took a few steps toward us. Then he turned to Demetrius and said, "Bring it in."

The Dracula lookalike reluctantly left Morgan and slipped out of a side-door, returning with another throne as vulgar as the one Acheron was lounging on. It was only slightly smaller, and the wings were not cut from a griffin but a phoenix, giving me the impression they were about to burst into flames at any moment.

"You can't be serious," I said.

"Deadly," he said.

"You're delusional on so many levels. Why would I agree to that?" I stared at the throne, and the disgust must have shown on my face.

Acheron was still calm and confident. "Because it's the only way your family's lives will be spared."

"We'd rather die than see Jax on that throne," said my father.

"No one's dying," I lied.

Acheron snapped his gaze to mine. "So, you agree?"

"Every king needs a queen," said Demetrius, although he didn't seem too keen on the prospect of me filling that position. He still hadn't forgiven me for winning the battle in the Moonlit Chapel.

"You'll rule the Realm beside me," Acheron said. "You'll have everything you ever need. Riches and magic beyond measure."

I blinked at him, my mind whirring away. Murderer, torturer, destroyer. Did he really think I'd agree to it? "I thought you were power-hungry," I said. "But now I see you're actually insane."

He was expecting that answer, but was irritated nonetheless. "You're turning down the position of Queen of the Realm?" he asked. "Of wealth and power like you've never dreamed of?"

I was going to say, "*Wealth and power are overrated,*" but I had experience of neither.

"If I need to choose between committing to you or the Grim Reaper," I said, "the Reaper gets my hand."

Acheron clenched his jaw and blinked hard. "Fine," he said. "It's what we assumed." He clicked his fingers, and the phoenix-winged throne burst into flames behind him and burned with orange and purple flames. Light gray smoke rose and caressed the high ceiling.

"It's a shame that you're so myopic," he said. "That you can't see past our differences for long enough to see the advantages it would bring the Realm."

"I don't see any advantages," I said. "When I look at you, all I see is pain and destruction."

"Stupid girl," Acheron said. "I was offering you a way out. A way for you to help the people. A way for your family and friends to live."

"Life under the Silvano rule will not be worth living," I said. "So you nipped that problem right in the bud."

"I'm not offering you a chance to die," he said.

Of course he was going to keep me alive. He was going to keep me in the dungeon and siphon my blood as he'd done to my parents. I looked at them again, weak and wasted away. I imagined what I'd look like after twenty years in the maze, being farmed for my blood.

What had Lysander said to me? He had been trying to convince me to leave the kingdom. I wasn't afraid of dying, I said, and he replied: *It's a fate worse than death.*

"Tell me about my lineage," I said.

Acheron shrugged. "It doesn't matter anymore."

"I'll decide that," I said.

I'm sure he knew I was buying time. But he also knew that there was a band of ogre-like Hammerskins guarding the palace with AK47s. Even if Darick was out there, there was no way he would be able to get in.

"Have you ever wondered," Acheron said, "why I singled you out? Why I singled your parents out that day?"

"They told me. I'm a dhampyr." Even then I felt the taint in my blood.

He smiled, but his eyes were empty. "Yes. But you're not just *any dhampyr.*"

Land the plane, Acheron, I wanted to say. *Spit it out already.* Instead I bit my tongue and waited.

"You're an Abarim," he said.

I frowned at him. *What?* I looked at my parents and they nodded.

"Your mother's name is Simone Abarim. Daughter of Blimaex and Elize."

"I know Blimaex," I said to my mother. "He hired me on a case."

"He's still alive?" my mother said. Her chest swelled, and dad held her hand.

"Alive and well," I said. I thought of when I had visited his house and was taken in by how warm and homely it had felt, despite its size. I felt a rush of tenderness toward the old wizard, who I now knew was my grandfather. And again I felt the searing loss of years and years gone by and love lost. I imagined playing as a child in the Abarim Manor gardens, making daisy-chains, eating ice cream on the generous verandah, and napping on the old stately couches.

"You destroyed an extremely valuable asset when you killed Slyden," Acheron said.

Good, I thought. At least I'd done something right. There I was, counting blessings again.

"The Abarim family has always been well respected," I said. "Blimaex was on the Council until Slyden attacked him."

"Yes," said Baldassare.

"But he has no blue blood. So why the harping on about my fancy lineage?"

"You really know nothing about your family," he said.

"How could I?" I demanded. "I grew up an orphan. A Copperfield chess piece."

"Your grandfather was an extremely powerful wizard in his day."

I imagined Blimaex, then, slinging spells and churning the skies with his staff. Battling demons and ogres and vampires. I looked at Acheron's scar, the one that ran from his hairline to his eye.

"He almost took my eye," said the vampire.

And then it made sense. I would be doubly valuable to Acheron because the blood that ran in my veins was the same as the wizard who had almost killed him. Not only did my heart pump potent blended wizard-vampire blood, but it was tinged with Acheron's virtual demise. Crimson gold.

The good news was that there was no way he was going to kill me. Not unless I tried to kill him, first, in which case he'd have no option. My best bet, I thought, was to get rid of his minions first. Hammerskins with itchy trigger fingers were probably the most immediate threat.

Before I could formulate a plan to deal with the Neo-Nazis, Acheron decided to move things along. Maybe he was tired of lounging, tired of talking, when none of it really mattered to him. Nothing mattered to him apart from my Magus and the Chaos Jar in my infinity pocket, and he had waited long enough.

CHAPTER 36
OVARIES OF STEEL

"I'm guessing you know what comes next," said Acheron.

Demetrius put his hand on Morgan's shoulder, and she shifted in her seat and moaned. I felt helpless, because I knew it was going to be an impossible decision.

I enter into an unholy alliance with Acheron—as Slyden had done—or Morgan would be killed. It was one thing to boast that I'd rather die than make a deal with the devil, it was totally different knowing that Morgan's life hung in the balance, and seeing Demetrius's filthy hand on her made me flare with anger.

"Give me the Jar," Acheron said.

I shook my head. "No."

No way. Uniting the three elemental fragments—one of which he already wore on his head—would give him enough power to raze the entire Realm, which I was pretty sure was the first thing on his agenda.

"I'm going to make this easy for you," he said. "Give me the Jar, or I'll kill your friends and family. Starting with this one," he gestured toward Morgan, who started to struggle again. "Demetrius has had his eye on her for hours, and he's very hungry."

"If you touch her," I said to Demetrius, my eyes narrowed. "I'll spear you with a lightning bolt. And I'll make sure it hits you where it'll hurt most."

Demetrius hissed at me, showing me his disgusting stained fangs.

"Give me the Chaos Jar," said Acheron, "and I'll let you all go."

"No."

He was getting agitated. "Last chance."

"Not going to happen," I said.

Demetrius crept closer to Morgan, gently moving her hair out of the way, exposing her neck. Morgan was fighting against her restraints, but she wasn't going anywhere. Fright painted my insides cold. It was like my nightmare was coming true, and there was nothing I could do about it. I knew how this dream ended. I felt for the Jar in my pocket.

"Fine," Acheron nodded at Demetrius. "Go ahead."

The vampire lifted his head and took a bunch of Morgan's hair in his fist, ready to plunge his fangs into her.

"Stop!" I shouted. "Wait."

Acheron looked at me expectantly. Demetrius appeared irritated.

"Yes?" he said.

I didn't know what to say. I couldn't give them the Jar, and without it I didn't have any leverage at all.

"I'm waiting," said Baldassare, his face beginning to flush with anger or excitement, I wasn't sure which. It highlighted his jagged scar.

As I stood there, bumbling, trying to think of something, the sounds that had been coming from outside came closer. We heard voices from the other side of the giant carved door, and then a loud knocking.

"Stay out!" shouted Acheron.

The knocking became more persistent.

"I said stay out!" shouted Acheron. His greased hair fell forward in his face, and he smoothed it back slowly, carefully, as if trying to keep his cool.

A small movement behind him caught my eye. It was high up, small. Black. A raven sat on a sill, watching us.

The persistent knockers didn't seem to know or care that Acheron had said not to enter. We heard the timber plank being slid away and the doors being pushed open.

"Sorry, your majesty," said one of the skinhead guards. "We told her to stay out, but—"

Shagar Khargol, baby strapped to her chest, strode into the room.

"Hello, Acheron," she said.

The vampire blinked in disbelief, as did I.

Sugar? How the faex—?

"I said stay out!" yelled Acheron at the guard.

I stared at her. Could she not have left the baby in a safer place before embarking on this *hara-kiri?*

"She insisted," said the guard.

"She insisted?" sneered Acheron. "She looks unarmed to me. And you have bullets in those things hanging around your necks, don't you?"

The guard looked at the floor, embarrassed by his empathy. I guessed that he hadn't shot Shagar because she was carrying a baby, and now he was going to pay for it. I tried to spot Gnor in his black cap, but I couldn't see him.

"I need a word," said Sugar. Her face was alight with purpose. I had such mixed feelings for the orc. Respect and revulsion in equal measure. Typical of Sugar Shagar to just walk into the New Dawn castle as if she owned it. The orc had ovaries of steel, that was for sure.

The commander general stood to attention. "Get her out of here!" he frothed.

"I'm in the middle of something," said Acheron. "Can it wait?"

I wondered, briefly, if I should just reach for my crossbow and try to get a shot in while Acheron was distracted, but something told me that wouldn't end well. Instead I'd try to be patient, and see what the Orc Godmother had to say.

Morgan had stopped struggling again, and she watched Sugar intently as she walked right up to Acheron. The orc lifted the phone in her hand, the same phone she'd put on the table during her negotiations with Raguk Magra.

"No," said Shagar. "It can't wait. Not unless you're happy to be surrounded by vipers." She sent a barbed look over to the general, who seethed and snarled at her.

"What?" said Acheron.

"I have something for you," she told him, and shook her phone. "Something I'm sure you'll find very interesting."

"What is it, then?"

Sugar looked at the screen and tapped it. Her volume was on full blast.

"...*THAT WAS THE DEAL,*" we all heard Raguk's recorded voice say. "*I help them seize power of the Realm, and they will ensure I keep my position, amongst some other ... perks.*"

I recognized the conversation immediately. I remembered Shagar going down on her hands and knees to light the fire in Raguk Magra's stonewalled sanctum at Alcazar. How the room had transformed from a cold, depressing place, to a cozy den.

There was the sound of Shagar's baby mewling, and I remembered how I, in a convincing orc glamour, had swayed and shushed the baby, playing my part as the Khargol wet nurse, while the phone Shagar had placed on the table between them had recorded everything they said.

We all listened to the recording with bated breath.

"You've made a deal with the Silvano clan, but that doesn't mean you need to honor it," said Shagar.

Raguk grunted. *"If I don't honor it I'll die an ugly death."*

"I think there is a new deal to be made."

There was a slight pause, then Magra said, *"I'm listening."*

"My men will stand down, the bombs will be defused."

"A truce," said Magra.

Acheron grew stone-faced as he listened.

"Better than a truce," she said. *"Because with our combined forces, we'll be stronger than the enemy."*

We heard Magra grunt in approval.

"Raguk," said Shagar's voice. *"Raguk. Do you understand what I am saying? If we join forces, we can defeat the Silvanos, and any other vampires who stand in our way."*

There was another pause, then Raguk cleared his throat. "*It's a good plan,*" he said.

A shuffling sound as Shagar stepped up to him. "*Deal?*"

Magra's chair scraped the ground as he stood. His voice was gruff. "*Deal.*"

WHEN THE RECORDING WAS OVER, Sugar slipped the phone back into her bag. Acheron whirled around to the commander general, his cape flaring.

"You," he growled. "Hammerskins!"

The general's eyes widened. "It was Magra. He was a fool. I would never have agreed to—"

Sugar watched as the vampire advanced on the general. "I knew you couldn't be trusted!" he shouted.

"It's her you should be wary of," the general said, narrowing his eyes at Shagar. "She's the one who led Raguk astray."

"You're saying that a *woman* with a *baby* managed to turn the whole army against me?"

"We're not against you," he said.

The Hammerskins in the room looked worried. They backpedaled slowly, trying to escape from the room without being noticed.

"Kill them," Acheron said to Demetrius, who looked shocked at the prospect. "Kill them all. I don't want to see one Hammerskin left standing."

"But, sir," said Demetrius. "These are the only Hammerskins left in the Realm. If you kill them, the castle will be left vulnerable. There are not enough of us to protect you."

Acheron looked angry enough to spit. "I'd rather have an unguarded castle than one protected by traitors."

Demetrius tried again. "Sir. These men did not turn on you. Don't punish them and yourself for a moment of weakness shown by their former leader."

Acheron clenched his jaw. "Kill. Them. All."

THE VAMPIRES ATTACKED the Hammerskins in the room, slashing their throats with their razor fangs before the orcs had a chance to scream or pull their triggers. Then they dragged them outside in search for the other guards and sentinels. I hoped that Gnor had managed to get away in time.

"What about her?" Demetrius asked, wiping blood from his lips and then pointing his stained fingers at Shagar. The Commander General lay beside him, bleeding out. "She's the one who turned Magra."

There was the sound of AK47s being fired outside, and bodies falling.

"Magra was ready to turn," said Acheron. "His heart was never in it. She was just the catalyst. We should thank her, really, for confirming what I already know. That the Hammerskins are a band of stupid, disloyal oafs who I no longer have any use for."

"But the castle is wide open now," said Demetrius.

"We have the HighFire Crown, Demetrius," said Acheron. "And soon we'll have the Chaos Jar, and the most potent Magus in the Realm. We don't need protection anymore. We don't need anything apart from what's in that wizard's pocket."

CHAPTER 37
A BLUR OF VIOLENCE

Acheron strode up to me, and I took a step back. He was a big man, strong and solid, and made more powerful by the Crown on his head. The vampire reeked of all the evil things he had done. He shoved his hand out toward me.

"Give it to me," he said, his sharp fingers curling like claws. Danger vibrated in the air around us; an electric storm cloud about to burst. I could tell he was trying to keep calm, but he was growing impatient. He'd worked long and hard for this moment, and there was no way he was going to give up the payoff.

"Give it to me!" he yelled.

"Never!" I shouted back.

The vampires who had been outside killing the guards flew back into the room, their chins shining with greasy orc blood.

"Kill the cop," Acheron said to Demetrius. Before I had time to think of how to stop them, Demetrius was at Morgan's throat. In a blur of violence he sank his teeth into her and she shouted in horror. It was exactly like my dream.

No! This couldn't be happening.

I saw the pleasure in Demetrius's body language, his wilting under the pure rapture of it, and I screamed and tried to run to her, but Acheron blocked my way.

"Kill them, too," said Acheron, pointing at my parents, who were cowering against the wall behind me. They had their magical tools out, but they were so weak, I knew they wouldn't stand a chance.

"No!" I shouted, but then the coven of greasy-lipped vampires was already on top of them, feasting. Mom's wand had dropped out of her hand and rolled away from her. I felt a sob rising and forced my hysteria down. I looked at Morgan again, and she had passed out. Demetrius continued to drain her body of blood, and I knew then that we were all going to die.

"I can give the command for them to stop at any time," said Acheron, licking perspiration off his upper lip. "It's not too late to save them. Just give me the Jar."

His hand was out again, grasping for the thing he needed so desperately to activate the New Dawn.

I couldn't stand it. I knew it would be suicide handing over the Jar. Worse than suicide. It would be apocalyptic. But I couldn't let my parents die after just finding them after all these years. I just couldn't. Consequences be damned, I needed my mom and dad. And there's no way I was going to let my best friend die at the hands of that repulsive creature at her throat.

"All right," I screamed. "All right!" I reached into my pocket and pulled out the Chaos Jar.

"Wizard, no!" yelled Shagar, marching over, but it was too late. The Jar had already been grabbed out of my trembling hands. Acheron grasped the glass container, and the blue lightning inside lit up his face, which was pulled into a kind of gleeful grimace. He looked insane.

"Stop them," I said to him. "Stop them!" But Acheron was so taken with his new toy that everything else disappeared. He had never intended to call his minions off. I'd have to do the honors. I scooped my mother's wand off the floor.

"*Fiat fulgur!*" I yelled, and a javelin of electricity shot out of the silver spell stick and speared Demetrius in his money-maker. He screamed and fell backwards, clutching his tool-box. Morgan slumped against her bonds, her eyes shut, her mouth slack. I spun around and slung the same spell at the vampires attacking my parents.

"*Fiat fulgur!*" Using both hands this time, I delivered two bolts of lightning, blowing the attackers away. They were thrown off their victims, but immediately tried to recommence. I blasted them again, and with an explosion of blue light they hit the floor and didn't get up again. My parents were both bloody and unconscious. When I turned to face

Acheron again, he had moved away from me and was heading toward his throne.

"Get me the Magus," he commanded of no one in particular.

Another round of vampires lowered themselves to our level, ready to attack. One female vampire in particular had her sights set on me. *"Ignem exquiris!"* I shouted, and a comet of fire barreled toward her. She dodged it just in time. The only damage caused was a small flame on her cape, which she batted off with an annoyed expression on her face.

"Wizard," she said. "You killed my sister."

"Entirely possible," I said.

"Her name was Desdemona."

Yes, I remembered her. The vampire with twin black whirlpools for eyes who liked to kill the clientele at The Jupiter Drawing Room. I remembered pink boxer shorts death-gurgling on the bed. She'd escaped that first night, but had my scent. She tracked me down the next evening with a couple of wingmen and tried to end it. Stole my bike and when I conjured it back, there she was, sitting astride it, in all her bloodsucking glory.

"I remember your sister," I said. "I remember how she died."

The vampire hissed at me, showing me her ivory fangs. I sent another blast of fire her way, then followed it up with a lightning bolt. She dodged both.

"You'll be reunited, soon," I said. I grabbed my crossbow from my back and whispered, *"Glaciem exquiris."* I pulled the trigger and the bolt shot out, flying through the air between us and freezing as it did so. The long, sharp spear of ice pierced Desdemona's sister right in the middle of her chest. Her eyes widened, her mouth was a black hole. The residual ice magic traveled into her body and froze her torso all around the arrow, and she dropped to the floor and shattered into ice shards, then the shards turned to ash.

I had no time to celebrate the victory. A vampire was at Sugar's throat. I couldn't sling a spell; the chances of hitting the baby were too high. I sprinted over to her and delivered a running kick to the vampire's jaw. There was a cracking sound of the bone breaking, and he fell backwards, disoriented, letting go of mother and baby. Before he had time to get back up I pulled my trigger and sent an arrow into his heart. He laid back, wrapped his fingers around the shaft of the bolt and blood began to bubble out of his mouth. I didn't watch him turn to ash; I had another trio of vamps to deal with. They rushed at me, hissing, and the air turned black with their capes. I pointed my crossbow at them and fired, yelling *"Insidia!"*

The bolt that left my crossbow changed, mid-air, into a snare-net and caught all three vampires before they could reach me. They struggled against the net and fell to the stone floor.

Sugar Shagar was untying Morgan, who was still bleeding, and still unconscious. Acheron was back on his throne, waiting for the third elemental fragment to be delivered to him.

I raced back to my parents, but before I could reach them, Demetrius caught my arm. He had been burnt by my magic, and his body language told me that he was in pain. The blood on his face repulsed me.

"We have to get out of here!" yelled Shagar, hoisting Morgan onto her shoulder. "Now!"

I looked back at my unconscious parents, then at Demetrius. There were still dozens of vampires in the way. I wouldn't be able to drag my parents out and fend off vampires at the same time. Demetrius breathed his disgusting metallic breath in my face. His fingers increased their grip on my arm, and he flew towards Acheron with me, like a black-feathered eagle clutching its prey.

"You asked for Magus," said Demetrius to his king.

Acheron looked at me, his eyes drilling into mine. "Perfect," he said. He lifted his head and opened his mouth, ready to strike. I saw his fangs. The fangs that had been the source of hundreds and hundreds of childhood nightmares, and I was right there, about to be bled into oblivion.

"No!" I shouted, trying to squirm out of Demetrius's grip as he handed me over to Acheron, but the men were stronger than I was. They both held on to me, making sure I couldn't escape. I tried to whip my crossbow up to Acheron's chest but he backhanded the weapon and it went clattering to the ground. I looked around for help but Sugar was now surrounded by the enemy.

Acheron looked at my throat, ready to strike, ready to deliver his ultimate *coup de grace*. It would have been a most fitting ending to the story, I thought. Killing the granddaughter of the wizard who had almost killed him; the granddaughter whose veins ran with the very thing he needed to create the black fire that would destroy the Realm. How perfect it would have been for Acheron, but I wasn't going to let it happen.

I kneed Demetrius in the balls, sending him collapsing forward, and then I kneed him in the face, smashing his nose. He cried out and let me go. Acheron lunged at me and his mouth travelled to my throat, but his teeth never reached my skin. I put my palm on his chest, over his old shriveled heart, and I thought of my parents lying there on the stone floor. The grief and fury was like a tornado rising, and I felt the power blasting through my arms and hands, eager to be released. Waves and waves of energy built up inside me.

"Fiat fulgur," I said. No one heard me, but all that the spell needed was that small flame and it exploded, blasting through my hand and zapping Acheron's heart. His body stiffened and shuddered as if I'd slid a Taser against his chest. As he fell back I grabbed the Jar, but another vampire snatched it from me before I could put it back into my pocket. I felt out of control and stunned by the ferocity of the magic I'd just pumped into Acheron's chest. Was he dead? I had no idea. There were still dozens of vampires to fight our way through, and at that moment it looked like I was the only one on the A-team standing.

"Ignem exquiris!" I shouted at the vamps huddled over Shagar, and the comet of blue fire knocked them off her. She stood up and gave me a quick nod of thanks. Gnor ran

through the doors carrying two automatic rifles, one of which he threw to Shagar. She caught it in one hand and strung it around her neck, the magazine resting on the baby she had strapped to her chest. She looked at me and yelled, "Behind you!"

I spun around. A snarling blood-stained vampire lurched toward me. I reached for my crossbow but remembered that Acheron had smacked it out of my hands. My hands were still burning from the fire and lightning spells.

"Glaciem exquiris!" I shouted, sending a shock wave of cold energy toward him, freezing him. It wouldn't last long. My energy was fading and the attackers kept coming, as if there was an infinite supply of vampires snaking out from the middle of the castle. My power wasn't going to last for long enough to dispatch them all. I suddenly felt overwhelmed. I looked over to the throne, where I had electrocuted Acheron. He was gone, and so was the Jar.

CHAPTER 38
ONE-HANDED WIZARDS

A vampire blurred in front of me and the shock of it knocked me backwards. I sprawled on the ground, cracking my elbow on the cold stone floor. He seemed to multiply before my eyes, and soon there were six of them, then ten, looking down at me with hungry expressions in their eyes. The sound of gunfire rang out, and bullets zinged through the air. Shagar and Gnor were shooting every vampire in sight. The creatures' bodies fell and ashed with colorful flames. The orcs didn't shoot at my attackers, perhaps worried they'd catch me in the crossfire. My mind was whirring, thinking of a spell that would be fatal enough to exterminate the creeps, but easy enough on my hands to save them for further magic. I had seen one-handed wizards before, and I had no wish to join their ranks.

The guns kept firing, and there was the smell of gunpowder and sparks in the air. It was a dangerous place to fire guns; the bullets ricocheted off the walls in all directions. One of the vampires surrounding me lunged, trying to grab me by the shoulders, but I screamed and punched him. I felt my knuckles crunch as they connected with his skull. He staggered backwards, and I shook out my hand, making a note to not punch any more vampires. It hurt me more than it hurt them. Another vamp went for me, and I dodged him just in time, but then two more stuck their hands out and soon they were all over me. I struggled against them, but there were too many. They began to cover me, and I felt like I was being pulled under by quicksand all over again. I battled to breathe. I began to panic. They were drawn even closer by my fear, and they closed in.

Forgetting my earlier resolution, I started to punch and kick as hard as I could, but the monstrous creatures just absorbed the blows and folded in further. I saw their ivory daggers and pictured them puncturing my throat. I screamed and fought, but they didn't let me go. My lungs were burning, desperate for air, and the panic and oxygen deprivation soon blinded me with a wash of silver stars.

SUDDENLY THE VAMPIRES starting shouting and thrashing, and I didn't understand what was happening. One by one they let go, and I lay gasping for air. I grabbed at my throat to check if I had been bitten, but there was no wound there, and as far as I could tell I was not bleeding. I looked up to see who had saved me, and there was Darick, in all his smoking hot vampire-killer glory. I probably imagined the golden aura around him, but in that moment it seemed real. Time slowed as he grabbed my hand and helped me up.

"Jax!" he said. "Are you okay?"

"Yes," I said, nodding. "Yes. But my parents... and Morgan—"

Darick looked over my shoulder at my unconscious parents.

"Don't worry about them. Their hearts are beating."

I don't know what kind of magical powers healing mages have, to be able to see from a distance if someone is alive or dead, but I was comforted by it.

"I can help them," said Darick, "but we need to get out of here."

I wanted to ask how he had found me, but we didn't have time to talk, and the answer happened to bowl along the floor and jump into my arms; a rolling ball of magical albino ferret fluff.

"Gizmo!" I said, hugging him and slipping him into my pocket. I had the intense urge to get out of there and find a place where Darick could heal my parents and Morgan. I looked around and saw no more vampires. Some had been killed; the rest had disappeared back to where they had come from.

"Shagar!" I shouted. "Gnor! Let's go!"

But Shagar shook her head. "We can't leave without the Jar."

She laid Morgan's limp body down with my parents.

My head exploded with Latin curse words. "We don't know where it is!"

On cue, Gizmo popped his head out of my pocket and pointed his nose toward the back of the hall. I sighed the sigh of a hundred female wizards who have just been told it was not good enough to just save their parents and save their best friend. They had to save the whole *faexing* Realm before they could go home for a nap.

Darick looked at me, and I nodded to the back of the hall. "Let's go."

CHAPTER 39
SYRUP THE COLOR OF MIDNIGHT

Gizmo led us toward the back of the hall and through a door. I tried to lead, but Gnor pushed ahead of me. He had the AK47, so I didn't argue. The raven swooped down and landed on my shoulder.

"Bron," I whispered, and he clicked his beak at me. I was glad he had found me, and I renewed my promise to find a way to break the hex that was keeping him in his raven form. We walked through a long dark stone passage lit by floating gaslights; strode deep into the castle innards until I could smell Acheron again, the yellow, sour stink of his evil. I guessed we were getting close to his chamber, and I swallowed hard. I didn't feel equipped to deal with what was going to happen next. I was spell-shocked and my magic was running low. I couldn't help thinking we were walking into a trap.

When we reached a T-junction, Gizmo squeaked for us to turn right, and then left. We came to a black wooden door with a quaint bronze doorknob. My speciality.

Door number one, I thought. *Let's have some fun.*

I put my hand on the engraved doorknob. *"Ignem exquiris,"* I said, and the warmth from my palm melted the handle just enough to compromise the bolt. I turned it, and the door opened. There was the scent of charred wood in the air.

It's difficult to explain what Acheron's chamber was like. I had expected a regal-looking den decorated with oriental carpets and classic gold-framed art. A blazing fire in the hearth. But the chamber was something you *felt* instead of saw. It was like a cube-shaped vacuum with permeable edges. It was the heart of the pocket realm: a soft block of negative space in the very center of the New Dawn Kingdom. You could see the vestiges of a den if you looked in one place for long enough, but it was all very nebulous. For the first time, I understood how solid ground and walls made one feel secure, because there in Acheron's chamber nothing was solid, or certain, or safe. It was like being in outer space, and constantly afraid you'd float away, psychologically speaking.

I understood then how dead people were alive in this pocket realm, and how he bent the laws of the micro-universe to his will. Most of all, I felt the same thick molasses-air swirling around us that I had experienced at EverShade. Evil so thick you could feel it slowing your steps. Syrup the color of midnight. I grasped Darick's hand, and his warm skin comforted me. At least he was real. I felt the presence of Sugar and Gnor, too, but they were hazy.

. . .

ACHERON WAS THERE, wearing his crown and looking larger than life again. He looked strong, and invincible, and it made me think of how ill and drained my parents were and the anger climbed. It was so fierce this time, and magnified by the atmosphere, that I felt as if the hatred was strangling me, and making me feel weaker rather than more powerful.

"Give us the Jar," said Shagar, but it sounded as if she was speaking under water.

Acheron laughed, which made my anger choke me more. Darick squeezed my hand and frowned at me as if to ask me if I was okay, and I tried to pull myself together. Suddenly he froze and let go of my hand. His face was a mask of shock.

"What is it?" I asked, but my words came out in puddles.

"Your parents," he said in slow motion. "Their hearts ... stopped beating."

CHAPTER 40

MAGICAL RUSSIAN ROULETTE

I wanted to rush back toward the hall; toward my parents. My first aid skills were sketchy, but I knew how to do CPR. I could take Darick with me. When I turned to go, the doorway was no longer behind me. There was no way out.

"Let me out," I warbled.

"Give us the Jar," said Sugar in slow motion.

We were under the thick gelatinous air and it was hard to move, but Acheron seemed undisturbed by the strange upside-down atmosphere. I needed to stop thinking of myself as the victim and start fighting back. I needed to be able to talk and move and breathe so that I could break out of the black heart of the kingdom and get to my parents. I kept hearing Darick's words echoing in my head.

Their hearts stopped beating.

Their hearts stopped beating.

Their hearts stopped beating.

No! I was not going to let this happen. The grief that welled up inside me was deep, dark, and awful. The magic it created was so potent that I could feel it burning in my chest.

"Ventum exquiris!" I shouted, and a warm wind rose. "Hold on!"

With my mother's wand I whipped up the wind. *"Ventum, ventum!"*

I kept stirring it up until it became a black tornado. It hungrily sucked up the soupy air that surrounded us, and glittered with it as it spun. I slung the tornado up to the ceiling of shadows. I used all my strength, trying to get it as far away from us as possible.

"Glaciem exquiris!" A thin streak of freezing energy traveled from the wand to the tornado and froze it there. It wouldn't last long, but at least we had a few minutes to breathe, and do battle. I was overflowing with magic, and I felt the sparks everywhere under my skin. If I didn't expel the forceful magic, I'd explode. I pulsed my fingers, trying to get rid of the icy feeling.

Acheron stood there holding the Chaos Jar, the golden High-Fire Crown on his head winking in the strange ethereal light. His eyes flamed in my direction.

"Come to me," he said, holding out his hand. "Come to me."

It became clear. I needed to sacrifice myself to save the Realm and everyone in it. I took a step forward.

"No," said Sugar. Gnor tried to block my way. Bron clawed my shoulder and shrieked.

"Come," said Acheron again, and I took another step toward him. Darick tried to pull me back, but I shook him off. I was being called to a higher purpose. I needed to go to Acheron.

"Jax!" said a voice behind me. The voice of a person I loved more than anything. It broke the spell. I spun around and blinked. Ferra and Fighour Fernak stood there in their full dwarven battle gear: Viking helmets, full body armor, and magical dwarven axes that glinted like the smiles on their faces.

"Ferra!"

I was so happy to see her that tears sprang to my eyes. She yelled "Catch!" and threw my crossbow to me. She had come through the hall and seen the wreckage there. The destruction, the bodies. I tried to swallow the ache in my throat. I couldn't believe I'd lost my parents again. I didn't have time to give in to the anguish. I needed to use it to destroy Acheron and his sick, nefarious realm. What better place to torpedo the New Dawn Kingdom than right here, in its small black heart?

The Fernaks advanced on Acheron. A wave of vampires, previously camouflaged by the dark, indistinct walls, came forward to stop them. I looked down at my hands, still stiff and blue from the previous spell. I caught sight of Lou's djinn stone, and I quickly rubbed it. Who knew if she'd be able to find us here, but it was worth a try.

Ferra shouted something in Dwarvish, some kind of battle cry, and began swinging her axe at the vampires. Fig did the same. Gnor and Sugar opened fire. The vampires hissed and screamed and ashed with multicolored sparks, and the air was thick with their blended, bitter smoke. Darick joined the Fernaks with a mixture of hand-to-hand combat and the whistling bullets of his pistol.

I felt a cold hand on my neck, and I jumped. It was Demetrius. He was about to sink a jugular hook into my neck when I elbowed him hard in the face. I felt his cartilage smash under the force of my arm, and he staggered backwards. I thought of what he had done to Morgan and the fury almost lifted me into the air.

I WAS afraid of the Death Spell, and rightly so. The chances of killing yourself by slinging one are extremely high. Think of a magical version of Russian Roulette with the gun pointing toward yourself and your target at the same time. Would you pull the trigger? Now think of that happening when you're pinned to a large spinning board and you're trying to throw knives but they keep heading in your direction instead of your enemy's. You're trying to control the knives but you're also trying to fire the gun, knowing full well that the barrel is primed and the trigger is just waiting for half an inch before exploding that keen bullet into your face. Would you pull the trigger? In most cases, your enemy doesn't warrant the risk posed to your own life. But Demetrius had hurt Morgan, and I was as mad as hell.

I thought of the trigger, and the unstable magic roiling inside me, and my common sense won out. I decided against it. But I could still *rumpis* the *filius canis.*

"Rumpis!" I shouted, and shoved my hands toward the vampire. The destruction spell caught him off-guard; he had been so intent on my throat he had lost sight of the fact that I was a kick-ass wizard. The first spell barreled into his arm, and I heard the bone break. It sounded like a gunshot. *"Rumpis!"* I shouted again, and the second spell flew into his stomach, which doubled him over and caused blood to spill from his mouth. I took a deep breath. *"Rumpis!"* I directed the final spell to his upper torso, and he grabbed his chest and fell over, and finally disintegrated into glowing cinders and ash. I can't say that I wasn't happy to smell that smoke.

When I looked up, I saw Darick and the dwarfs still fighting, and the orcs emptied the last of their ammunition into the constant waves of attacking vamps. I didn't understand where they were all coming from. It was as if Acheron had an infinite supply of cannon fodder. There was a blast of white smoke, and Lou appeared. She looked incredible with her dark skin and quinine eyes, like some kind of warrior princess. I looked at her and nodded my thanks. Without saying anything, she took in the scene and drew her djinn blade. The first vampire who approached her lost his head, literally.

Next, Isadora Crowe ran in, followed by Laurent, her werewolf beau. Izzy immediately began turning the vampires to ash with her witchcraft, which I knew from experience was elegant, and deadly. Laurent shifted into a wolf and pounced on the attacker closest to him, tearing open his throat.

The Belore twins arrived next. I wanted to tell them to leave, that it was too dangerous, but the entrance sealed up behind them as it had done to me. There was nowhere to go, even if they'd agree, which I was sure they wouldn't. I could see in their shimmering eyes that they wanted to avenge their parents' deaths. They were holding Ametrix's Dragon's Eye amulet. Eafaris and Pepin were children and had no place there, but I welcomed their powerful combined magic. The twins looked at me, and I nodded. They held hands, ready to fight.

CHAPTER 41
ICE & VENOM

My friends fought off the attackers, which meant I could focus on Acheron. I remembered the spell I had used to angle Gizmo away from Zargulg that day I rescued him from the cage-fighting at the SubRealm beer hall. I had flung my magic up and across, like a fly fisherman, and hooked the ferret with the magical line before reeling him in.

It wasn't without danger. If I dropped the Jar and it cracked further, who knew what sinister things would leak out of the Void. It was a reckless strategy, but it was the only one I had.

"Volas!" I shouted, and I threw my line out toward the Jar in Acheron's grip. It wrapped around the glass, snatching it from his hands. It traveled in the air toward me, and I caught it, then quickly slipped it back inside my trench coat. Acheron bellowed in anger, and came toward me.

I looked around at the battling forces and saw that our team was getting tired. The onslaught of vampires seemed endless, and we wouldn't be able to keep them at bay for much longer.

Acheron was chanting something under his breath, and his eyes were rolling back. I couldn't hear the exact words, but it sounded something like a conjuring spell.

There was a huge ripple of energy, as if someone had dropped a rock into the pond which was the floor. Out of the ripple rose a ghost in a wizard's robe. At first I thought, *thank the Void!* An experienced wizard could help us defeat the Silvano army. But then the ghost turned to me, and I saw his face. This was no rescue mission. This was the specter that Acheron had conjured. Chalky skin, black capillaries snaking out from his hollow eye sockets. My blood froze. He was the most evil wizard I knew. Slyden Abarim.

"Hello, great-uncle," I said.

He looked confused, but held up his staff, anyway. With a sharp hit of adrenaline I realized that as he was ghost, he'd have no fear of using a Death Spell.

"Obeis diem supremum," he chanted in a deep, resonant voice.

Yep, it was the Death Spell, and I was unarmed. Holy hex. I was dead meat.

"Tempus est tibi," he said.

I saw the spectral magic swirling around the snakehead of his staff. I took a breath and braced myself.

"Nunc defungor!" he shouted, and shot his staff out at me.

The spell darted toward me, and I was ready for it. *"Effectus aversum!"* I shouted. I batted the spell away from my body and straight back at Slyden. I waited hopefully for his yell of pain, but the magic just went rippling right through him. Just as I had thought. You can't kill a ghost. *Faex.* This was no small problem.

IMMEDIATELY HE SLUNG a new fatal spell at me, and I countered it again, but this time it touched the back of my hand. The pain was like nothing I'd ever felt before. It was like getting hit with a poisonous lightning bolt. It burned and froze at the same time. My knuckles felt like they were melting, and the residual toxic magic left a pricking sensation as if stinging nettles had been sewn under my skin. I exclaimed in pain and tried to shake it out, but the movement only made the pain worse. The bones in my hand were fractured and barbed, and cutting into my flesh. I cried out again, I couldn't help it.

The ghost wizard was ready to sling a third killer spell, and I knew I wouldn't be able to defend myself against it. Slyden knew it, too. He raised himself to his full height, his robe fluttering out around him, and he pointed his staff at me.

"Obeis diem supremum," he began. I had three seconds before he skewered me with a spell that would send me on a one-way antique steam train to Halloween Heaven. The shooting pain in my hand was so intense I thought for a moment that death may, in fact, be preferable to living with that kind of agony. I bit my tongue. I wouldn't cry out again; wouldn't give him the satisfaction.

"*Tempus est tibi*," he said, and that sinister ghostly magic rippled around the staff.

I remembered the Jar in my pocket. If Slyden demolished me, he'd destroy the Chaos Jar, too, and I couldn't let that happen.

"*Nunc defungor!*" he shouted, and the force field of death came rocketing toward me.

I suddenly felt Pepin and Eafaris by my side. I was worried for them, but there was nothing I could do.

"*Clipeum glaciei,*" they yelled in unison, holding the amulet out. From the Dragon's Eye swirled a wall of water between Slyden and us, and it turned to a thick shield of ice. The Death Spell smashed into it, shattering the wall into thousands of pieces that scattered all over the floor in sharp glass rocks.

I looked at the Belore twins, my mouth slack with surprise. They had just saved my life.

"SLYDEN," came a voice from the other side of the chamber. The twins and I turned to look at where the voice was coming from. It was the yang to Slyden's yin. The Good Wizard.

"Blimaex," I whispered. Now that I knew he was my grandfather I noticed the subtle similarities in our faces, and our bodies. He seemed to glow with his latent power, and I felt honored to be related to him.

I couldn't see them, but I knew that Blimaex Abarim still had the scars from when his brother used Contagious Magic to carve the Latin fairy tale into his skin. Blimaex had almost died at the hands of Slyden's dark magic.

"Brother," sneered Slyden. "Get out of my way. This doesn't concern you."

"On the contrary," said Blimaex, standing in the way, his robe flowing around in front of me, sheltering me from Slyden's view. "It concerns me very much."

Blimaex was radiating a kind of ice-blue magic, and Slyden a hint of poisonous green. Ice against venom. Living opposing dead. Good versus evil.

I was so grateful that Blimaex had risked his safety to come through the portal to help us. I was scared stiff by Slyden when he was alive, but now that he was dead he seemed even more terrifying. And invincible.

"Res ac mortales salarium!" shouted Blimaex, swinging his staff around in one hand. The motion of the magical stick painted the air green. Something else appeared in his other hand, but I couldn't see what it was beyond seeing a pile of white powder. Slyden shouted out his own spell, which I didn't hear over Blimaex's, and they both sent their magic toward each other, clashing in the middle, ice and venom. While their currents were smashing into one another, and both men were exclaiming from the effort it took, Blimaex threw the white grains at Slyden.

The phantom started screaming. He dropped his snake-head staff and began clawing at his skin. Of course, it was salt.

Salarium. It was one of those things you learn in Supernatural Self-Defense at the Copperfield Institute and forget the day after you write the theoretical exam. Which was a shame, really, in my profession, because I could have warded off a lot of nasties just be reaching for the salt cellar. One of the reasons I've never really fitted in with other wizards is because they always seem to be studying the texts, while I prefer to focus on practical magic. Luckily Blimaex was the studious type.

Slyden's empty eye sockets were hissing and steaming, and his skin was melting off his skull. He was letting off the most disturbing scream I'd ever heard in my life. I felt it cutting into my ears, into my brain. Even though he was a ghost, I had to avert my eyes from the scene. It was gory and made the bile rise in my throat. I was pretty convinced Slyden would fade away into nothing, but he wasn't going to give up that easily. He shouted out a spell I didn't understand and smashed his fist into Blimaex's chest, and Blimaex went flying backwards, sprawling on the floor and losing his staff.

Eafaris ran to collect the staff and hand it back when Slyden side-swiped the boy with a *rumpis,* sending him flying to the other side of the room. Pepin ran to help her twin, leaving me exposed and vulnerable. Slyden opened his melting mouth and breathed a ghostly kind of green gassy fire in my direction, like a dragon from the Void. I scrambled back, so only the edges of the flames touched me. My skin sizzled and blistered. I was still nursing my wounded hand, and knew there was nothing I could do to fend the phantom off. I helped Blimaex off the ground, but he felt frail and weak in my arms.

I thought he looked so glorious when he arrived, thought he would save us all. Right then, feeling his thin arms through his cloak, I realized that he was just a wizard, no more, and no less. And no one was going to save me but myself.

CHAPTER 42

BLACK PETALS

That's when I realized we were going about the battle in the wrong way. Firstly, we were all fighting our own individual clashes, when we should have been fighting as a team. Secondly, Blimaex and I were trying to stop the phantom—which couldn't be killed —instead of trying to stop the conjurer of the phantom. Slyden had never been the ultimate enemy. Yes, he was the most maleficent wizard I had ever encountered, but that was because he had made a pact with the devil. The real devil was Acheron.

As Slyden lurched toward me, his skin still steaming, I shouted out to everyone.

"Together!" I yelled. "Together!"

How they knew what I meant, I'll never know. There was so much going on in that small dark heart of the realm, a surreal nightmare in 3D, but somehow they knew. As they kept fighting, slinging axes and smashing automatic rifles over heads and sinking deadly werewolf teeth into pale vampire skin, they also moved toward one another, and toward me, until we formed a chain of good versus evil.

I don't know why it took me so long to realize that, like the Belore twins, the only way to defeat a vampire as powerful as Acheron would be to combine our power. Eafy limped around the back of us and handed Blimaex back his staff. He took hold of Pepin's hand. Ferra and her husband, Fighour, also clasped each other's hands. Isadora Crowe and Laurent did the same. Darick felt for my injured hand and I winced as he squeezed it, but in an instant the pain was gone and the damage was undone. The tension in my body eased, allowing me to feel my magic again. Lou took Blimaex's hand, and Bron was on my shoulder. Shagar Khargol patted her baby with one hand and held Gnor's with the other. She had a look of pure determination on her face, jaw clenched, eyes like lasers. A mama bear who would strip the meat from a man before allowing him to touch a hair on her baby pickle's head. The couples all held hands, some romantic, some mismatched. Standing in that human chain we all joined up together, creating a blue force field to rival anything Acheron could throw at us, including his conjured specter of Slyden. We felt our combined power rushing through us and between us. The Silvanos stopped attacking. They held back, hissing and showing us their fangs. Slyden collapsed, and fell into a pile of salty bones.

Acheron snarled at us. As long as he had the Crown, he would win the day, and he knew it. He swept his arm across the room, sending out a hailstorm of green sparks. Blimaex shouted "*Protendo!*" and slammed the bottom of his staff into the ground, creating a barrier to protect us. A thin icy bubble shield repelled the hail of sparks, and they flew back in Acheron's direction. Angry, he sent another storm our way, and our shield not only protected us but actively thrust the sparks back at Acheron, and they landed on his teal cape, on his skin and hair. It seemed like a small victory, but it was not. All we were doing were defending ourselves, and that's not how you win a fight. I had been in enough scraps with the Ferals to know that.

This is the moment, I thought to myself. *This is the moment the war will be won or lost.*

Acheron and the Silvano Clan had used Blood Magic for centuries to build up the kind of power they had. Blood was fueling them, and I would use blood to defeat them. Blood Magic was my superpower; I had always used pain to augment my magic, and at that moment I had no shortage of it. My newly rediscovered parents lay dead in the hall, and my best friend was probably dead, too. I had killed my brother, Lysander, even though I wouldn't have been alive without him. I'd been numb to the grief earlier. The shock had stolen my grief and hidden it away, but I dug it up and allowed myself to feel the full weight of what had happened. The pain bloomed in my chest: the familiar giant charcoal rose. It grew and twisted open and showed off its cruel black petals. I felt every thorn, every stab in my swollen, aching heart. A sob wracked my chest, and with it my magic pulsed through my body like a live current, ready to strike. My whole body was just a vessel for that vast, terrible magic I felt inside, and I was ready to use it.

. . .

But there was something else. A different pain. There was something more powerful beneath the dark emotions. A silver shimmer. It made my heart ache just as much as the sorrow, but it was not sad. It came from seeing Ferra risk her life to help us fight, it came from seeing the twins face bravely terrors no children should ever see. It was the feeling of Darick's skin on mine, healing me over and over, inside and out. This feeling was even more potent than the pain, and I allowed it to rise inside me. I relinquished control over it, and it exploded into multiple layers.

I had thought that my pain would make me powerful enough to defeat Acheron, but I was wrong. It was the chain we had formed, our relationships and all that our relationships had brought along; our combined history of life and joy and hope and love. It contained all the meals that Ferra had cooked for me, the kindnesses Lou had extended me, the lessons I had taught Bron, and a hundred other things I couldn't name standing there facing Acheron; I felt it all, and I almost burst with the emotion and potency of the magic it brought.

It was go time, and I was ready.

The king of the New Dawn Kingdom was about to attack again when I whispered a command to Gizmo. The ferret nodded and cleaned his whiskers. I took a deep breath and braced myself.

CHAPTER 43

ASH AND BLOOD

G izmo rushed out of my pocket and flew at Acheron's head, grabbing the Crown and scuttling down behind him, disappearing into the dark edges of the room.

"No!" Acheron cried, his hands flying up to his head and pounding it in anger. "No!" Then he turned to his minions and yelled, "Kill them all!"

But the vampires were too afraid to attack us. They could see how powerful we were. The security of the castle had been breached, and we had all but destroyed their clan. Without the HighFire Crown they knew they were fighting a losing battle. They backed away, fraction by fraction.

Slowly, but also all at once, Acheron aged and wilted. He went from an upright vampire with muscles and glowing health to a bent-over old man with gray skin, and his eyes misted over with cataracts.

Acheron was dying before our eyes, and he was furious. "Kill them!" he shouted again. His voice was hoarse. There was the flashing of black and teal as the Silvanos ignored their leader, drew their capes, and left. Gizmo flew up my body with the Crown and disappeared into my pocket. We now had the Jar and the Crown, and we were safe from the elemental black fire that had the power to ruin the Realm. I thought of leaving, but I glanced at the scar on Acheron's forehead—which was so pronounced now without the healing magic of the Crown—and knew that I had to end Acheron's life or die trying.

It was my destiny as granddaughter of the wizard who almost succeeded in ending Acheron's life, and it was the destiny of the daughter of the parents he had so cruelly imprisoned and tortured for his own gain.

I broke the chain and stepped forward, and the friends behind me reached out and closed the gap. Their combined magic would protect me to a certain extent. Still, I was in trouble, and I knew it.

"Jax!" shouted Sugar. "Let's go!" But she didn't break rank, and their magic remained constant.

"Not before I make things right," I said. I knew that, old man or not, if I bowled a Death Spell at Acheron he'd swat it right back at me, and my spice cookies would be numbered. What I needed was something that would distract him enough so that he wouldn't be ready and waiting to counter that spell. I looked at the Belore twins, and they were clutching each other as well as their father's amulet, and Ferra shored them up with her sturdy arms. I looked at Darick, who nodded at me.

I have faith in you, his eyes said, *but don't* faex *it up.*

I inhaled a long, shaky breath. Was I really going to sling a Death Spell at the most powerful vampire in the Realm? I thought of the Russian Roulette and the spinning board; the sharpened silver knives.

Ah, well. Halloween Heaven couldn't be that bad, after all. I could do with some self-indulgent moaning and some candy. Maybe I'd come back as a ghost and haunt Morgan's house—in a friendly way, of course—or The Copper Cog & Ale. I could pour beers and stoke the roaring fire and poke bad tippers in the ribs.

Then I remembered what the Hammerskins had done to Ferra's pub, and the romantic ideal of phantasm lost its appeal. Nope, I wasn't going to die. If I could just work out a genius way to distract Acheron before—

As if Bron had read my thoughts, his sharp claws released my shoulder and he flew toward the vampire. I held my breath, not knowing what to expect. The raven flew directly into Acheron's face and before the vampire could swat him away, he plucked out one of Acheron's eyes and flew away. The vampire screamed and held his face as it bled. It was the same eye he had almost lost in his battle with Blimaex all those years ago. I didn't waste any time. I held my wand out toward Acheron and shouted. *"Obeis diem supremum, tempus est tibi, nuns defungor!"*

My Latin was rusty, but I knew I had gotten the incantation right, because all that magic I had swirling and boiling inside me left my body and hurled itself toward Acheron, smashing him in the chest and turning him stiff and pale. He had no vampires left to defend him, and no Crown to protect or heal him. His body turned into a stone statue and then cracked with neon green fissures. He burst open, exploding into a bright green bonfire like I'd never seen before, launching his body into the space all around us like a portal spell gone wrong. Would he be able to put himself back together if we left him like that? I wanted to stay to make sure he was dead and ashed, but I also understood that we had to leave right away or the heat of the blaze would incinerate us.

"Run!" shouted Shagar.

"We can't leave yet!" I shouted back.

"Trust me," said the orc.

Now, usually if someone says "trust me" it's a red flag of gigantic proportions, but the heat was unbearable, and we had no choice but to leave.

We backed away from the poisonous-looking bonfire and began to run through a new doorway Blimaex had created with his staff. We sprinted through the dark, damp passageway and landed up in the hall again, the floor of which was smeared in ash and blood. My parents' bodies lay there, as did Morgan's, and even I could see—without special healing mage powers—that their hearts were still. I stumbled and almost fell on top of them, the grief razing any rational thoughts.

"Don't worry," said Ferra, breathing hard.

I looked up at her, frowning. *Don't worry?*

"I put a heart-pause spell on them," she said. "I didn't think they'd make it, otherwise."

My head spun, but in a good way. Darick had sensed their hearts had stopped beating, but they were not dead. They were in a kind of magically induced coma, as Estelar Pavaris's phoenix had been when I had visited his mansion for the first time. When he had given up the Crown and started this terrible sequence of events. He was still clueless to it; he was prancing on the London Theatre stage, oblivious to the devastation he had wrought in the Realm.

"Don't worry," Ferra said again, helping me up. "I'll reverse it as soon as they're in the hospital. There's a place called Silver Wing that magically had some beds open up."

"Ferra," I said to her, so grateful I felt like weeping.

Fig hoisted my father onto his left shoulder, and Darick carried my mother and Morgan, but I knew that no matter how strong they were, they weren't going to make it all the way back. We raced out of the hall and found Quicksilver waiting for us, whinnying and snorting clouds of white vapor in the cold night air. We used my nano to strap my parents safely to the horse's back, and I stroked his elegant neck in gratitude. Lou commanded him with ease.

We were about to leave the castle grounds when Sugar turned and made her way back into the hall. I ran after her, even though every molecule in my body was telling me to run in the opposite direction, toward the people I loved. Toward home.

"Sugar! No!"

I followed her solid footsteps back through the hall that smelt of fire and death and through the cold stone passageway. There was a flash of foreboding, and I gulped down my fear. When we entered that horrible black cube again, Acheron was standing in the center, dusting himself off. The fire was gone. He looked old and withered, but he was alive. I couldn't believe it. Was it possible that he had amassed so much power from the Magus he had collected over the years that he could even survive a Death Spell? If so, what hope did we have?

Before I melted into a puddle right there, Shagar gave me a hardcore look, as if she was about to deliver one of her mean right hooks, but instead she unstrapped the baby from her chest and threw it at Acheron, who automatically caught it.

I was shocked and puzzled, and then I realized it wasn't Sugar's baby at all. It was a lifelike baby doll, and it had wires on its front.

I remembered something Sugar had said to Raguk Magra while she was negotiating their alliance. She had made the point that they had access to bombs and other explosives.

"For years we've had access to an underground military bunker," she had said to him. *"Left over from the last war. Forgotten by authorities."*

When I looked at Sugar again, I saw the flip switch on her chest. She hit the button, and we dived out of that strange upside-down chamber just before it was blown to smoking smithereens. The vacuuming nature of the room contained most of the blast. We sprinted away from it, all the while being hit with the heat and the debris. We left the small black heart of the New Dawn Kingdom to implode in on itself, and take the Silvano Clan's pocket realm with it. The castle grounds started to shimmer and crumble around us, and the green fire began to leap around and burn everything. Pictures fell from the walls and the teal banners scorched and shrunk as the flames devoured them.

We arrived outside again, gasping and panting. I pulled out my skeleton portal key and we all huddled around it while I chanted the best gateway spell I knew. As the magic lifted us into the air, I realized with a punch in the guts that Bron hadn't made it out. I wanted to stop the spell, but it was too late, and we were already flying through the gray flinty tunnel, on our way home.

EPILOGUE
SWEET DEATH-SPIRAL DREAM

It was our first Sunday lunch together.

It had been two weeks since we defeated Acheron and destroyed the New Dawn Kingdom, and things in the Realm were finally starting to feel like they were getting back to normal. A new kind of normal, anyway. One where I was no longer an orphan. Other things had changed, too. When the pocket realm exploded, so did the plant in my kitchen, which detonated my entire apartment and the seven floors below it. I was glad the voracious shop-of-horrors weed had spontaneously combusted, but I did feel sorry for my odiferous orc landlord. What would he do for a hobby, now that he didn't have me to chase for my always-overdue rent? So far I wasn't missing him, or the goblin-sized shower, or the flea-bitten furniture. To be honest, when Darick had taken me to the rubble to break the bad news, I had felt rather liberated. That's what happens when you realize you own nothing but the scorched and smelly clothes on your back. I felt my heart beating and my blood being pushed through my veins, and that was enough for me. Everything else was a bonus.

Another bonus was Darick inviting Gizmo and me to live with him. It had felt strange, at first. On one side we were strangers and knew nothing about one another, and on the other side we knew everything we needed to know. We were meant to be together. It was cheesy, but it was true. As Darick said to me, *"When you know, you know,"* and I felt the same way. Also, soulmate connections aside, living in his apartment was amazing. His fridge was always full, for one, and he had every gadget and comfort you could think of, yet the place remained super neat and spacious. Millionaire minimalism. Housekeeping cleaned the place daily and did the laundry, so it was a little like having Ghost around again, except they didn't slam hardcover books to the floor or scold me with cold patches of air if I skipped lunch or missed my curfew.

I LOOKED across the table at my father, and he winked at me. Mom saw us looking at each other and smiled, and Dad squeezed her hand. Sometimes I felt as if I was dreaming when I looked at them, or talked to them. Sometimes I thought I had actually died in the kingdom and this was just some kind of long, sweet death-spiral dream. But it wasn't. This was real. I knew it because I could feel Darick's warm hand on my thigh, and I could smell Ferra's cooking.

The Copper Cog & Ale was gradually being rebuilt, and was due to re-open by New Year's Eve. We had a huge launch party planned, but for now, a more relaxed lunch was what was needed. Blimaex had offered his house for the occasion; Abarim Manor at 44 Dresden Drive, and that is where we sat in his handsome dining room decorated with silver antiques and cream wallpaper and orchids. I was still getting used to the idea that we were related, but he made me feel very welcome. It was also good for Blimaex, who seemed to thrive in our company. He became more animated, and ever cheerful. I guessed that he had been very lonely before we showed up, having lost his parents and his daughter, rattling around in that big old house. Blimaex was also glad to be back on the freshly un-mesmerized Council. Willard, the butler, also seemed to have a new lease on life, and he buzzed around us happily refilling glasses and delivering trays of Ferra's delicious *hors d'oeuvres*. We were all buoyed by the knowledge that we had survived, and we had defeated evil.

We listened to the children's laughter that filtered in from outside. The whole Fernak tribe was there, as were the Belore twins, whom Ferra and Fighour had officially adopted. We could hear them laugh and shout as they ran around on Blimaex's vast emerald lawn, playing with Gizmo. They were thrilled with the secret passageways and garden nooks and the snowy owl. It would be just a matter of a year or so before Sugar and Gnarg's baby could join in the fun, but for now she was snoozing happily against Sugar's—non-trip-wired—chest.

And speaking of napping, there was a new addition to the security guards at Abarim Manor. Blimaex had hired Gnor, who now stood with the other guards at the entrance in a smart black uniform, waving visitors in—when he wasn't dozing in the sun.

. . .

Ferra stepped into the dining room, her cheeks flushed from the heat of the kitchen. She was balancing five large platters of food on her hands and arms; a balancing act any Cirque du Soleil artist would be proud of. As she laid the beautiful food before us, Willard charged our glasses with the Velour Brut he had chilled overnight. There was a golden beef Wellington with brown-butter potatoes, creamed spinach with toasted almond flakes, and cinnamon pumpkin pie baked to perfection. A steaming roast chicken with oregano and hazelnut stuffing, cauliflower gratin, and green beans sautéed in garlic, lemon and black pepper.

"You've outdone yourself," said Fig to his wife, which was no small compliment. We all clapped and agreed. Blimaex rose with his champagne flute, and cleared his throat. A hush fell on the room.

"I'll keep this short," he said.

"That'll be a first," said Willard, and everyone laughed.

"It would be a travesty to let this delicious food get cold, so I really will keep it to a few lines." He cleared his throat again. "To my dear daughter, Simone," he looked at my parents. I was still getting used to the idea of them having first names. "And Dex. We're so grateful that you're back in our lives." His voice cracked a little, but he recovered quickly. "I can't believe how lucky I am, getting not only my daughter back, and my son-in-law, but a beautiful granddaughter, too, who just happens to be one of the best wizards I know."

I blushed. I felt just as lucky, and my heart swelled.

"Hear, hear," said Morgan, raising her glass. I grinned at her. She could only join us for an hour, *"Just for a bite,"* she said, then she had to get back to Scorpion HQ. Musubarin had left the office in total disarray, and now that she was captain again, it was up to her to sort it out. Tilexon Musubarin was exactly where he belonged: in the Black Tower. In a satisfying twist of events, Morgan had been the one who arrested him. The Council had received Musubarin's laptop from an anonymous source—ahem, Pepin—and found all kinds of damning evidence on the hard drive, from communication with top Silvano vampires to evidence that tied him to Flint and the V-Cult murders. He'd be in the bony bowels of the Black Tower for a long, long time.

I had asked Lou to join us for lunch, but she had deferred the invitation. She was spending the day training Quicksilver, who I had given to her. She was a natural on horses, and the Void knew I owed her a favor or two. They were something to behold, the two of them. They moved perfectly together, as if they were one creature, an elegant mirage of silver and white smoke.

A surprise guest was Kim Smith, the nurse from Silver Wing. I was taken aback when I saw her arrive, wondering how she had found me, and what she was planning to do about the fact that I had commandeered her body for my own require-ments. But she wasn't there to see me; she didn't even recog-nize me. It was my parents who had invited her, to say thank you for the special care she took of them while they were recovering in the hospital. I gave her a tentative smile, and she returned it.

"You'll all be pleased to know that the Chaos Jar has been returned to the Council and has been hidden in a new place of safety. Many additional security measures have been put in place. And the HighFire Crown, well," Blimaex looked at Directress Copperfield, who was sitting at the opposite head of the table, "The Council has agreed to donate the crown to the Copperfield Institute, where it can be used to rebuild the premises and maintain its excellent standards in the education of our young witches and wizards, and keep them on the path of good magic."

"Oh, thank you," said the directress. "Thank you, Mister Abarim. You have no idea what that means to me." Everyone clapped and cheered, and sipped their champagne, which was crisp and delicious and not laced with Indigo Violent. I knew, because I had checked the color of the cork. What can I say? Paranoia has kept me alive and well.

"Really, thank you ever so much," said Copperfield, and fluttered her eyelashes at Blimaex.

I could have been imagining it, but I thought I might have seen a spark of chemistry between the two of them. Directress Copperfield looked perfectly placed, sitting at the head of Blimaex's long polished oak table. I looked at Isadora Crowe, who seemed to be thinking the same thing. She gave me a skewed smile, no doubt remembering the spiteful battles we had at school, like when she had cut off all my hair while I slept. At the time it had been the unfunniest joke in history. Beside her was Laurent, who looked at the food on the table and let out a low growl, and the werewolf in my stomach echoed it. It was time to tuck in.

Darick dished up food for me, and as I was about to take a bite, the doorbell rang. Willard, who had just sat down for the first time in hours, began to stand, but I put my hand out and told him I'd get it. Darick, stood, too, and said he'd come with me.

"You don't need to protect me," I said to him as soon as we left the dining room. "I can look after myself. Plus, there are security guards at the front gate."

"Gnor doesn't count," Darick said, and I laughed.

We were alone in the cool passage when he pushed me up against the wall and kissed me. A deep, gentle, passionate kiss that scored my insides and made my skin rustle with magic; my pelvis ached with longing.

"I know," he said, when he pulled away. "I know I don't need to protect you." He put his thumb on my bottom lip. "I just wanted to do that."

We walked together to the front door. When I opened it, my mouth fell open.

"Bron?" I said, and he nodded. He was in his human form, and his jade button eyes glinted mischievously at me. Happiness and relief washed over me. "But how?"

"The flames destroyed my feathers," he said.

It was all he needed to say. The supernatural fire must have released the raven hex. Nothing else mattered. We rushed into a hug and didn't let go for ages. I swiped my tears away and told him he'd better get inside before his food got cold. Darick closed the door against the warm afternoon light and the laughter of the children, and he smiled at me. I leaned forward into his body, kissing him deeply, and I felt the light silver sparks of magic all over my skin.

THE END

ALSO BY JT LAWRENCE

FICTION

WHEN TOMORROW CALLS

• SERIES •

(Futuristic kidnapping thriller)

The Stepford Florist: A Novelette

The Sigma Surrogate

1. Why You Were Taken

2. How We Found You

3. What Have We Done

When Tomorrow Calls Box Set: Books 1 - 3

(complete)

URBAN FANTASY

BLOOD MAGIC

(complete 6-book series)

1. The HighFire Crown

2. The Dream Drinker

3. The Witch Hunter

4. The Ember Isles

5. The Chaos Jar

6. The New Dawn Throne

CURSEBREAKER

(complete 6-book series)

1. The Dusk Reapers

2. The Haunted Portal

3. The EverShade Ring

4. The Obsidian Castle

5. The Pick Pocket's Curse

6. The Eternal Betrayal

❧

STANDALONE NOVELS

The Memory of Water

(steamy psychological thriller)

Grey Magic

(witchy magical realism)

EverDark

(urban fantasy)

❧

SHORT STORY COLLECTIONS

Sticky Fingers

Sticky Fingers 2

Sticky Fingers 3

Sticky Fingers 4

Sticky Fingers 5

Sticky Fingers 6

Sticky Fingers: The Complete Collection:
Books 1 - 6: 72 Short Stories

~

NON-FICTION

The Underachieving Ovary
(memoir)

The Indie Author Game Plan

~

www.ingramcontent.com/pod-product-compliance
Lightning Source LLC
Chambersburg PA
CBHW050604190726
48283CB00007B/2275